Ghost of Me

Amanda Steel

© 2019 Amanda Steel

Haunting my own life

I'm a ghost
Haunting my own life
Trying to remember
How not to be forgotten

I'm a ghost
But my heart still beats
Now I'm slowly fading
Soon there will be nothing left

I'm a ghost
Watching, listening, wishing
I was still part of something
While everyone else gets to live

I'm a ghost
Though I still have breath
Everything plays out in front of me
But it's all just out of reach

Prologue

He lurked in the shadows, waiting and hoping she wouldn't take a different route. This was her usual route. He knew that; he knew her. Obscured by the two looming buildings he stood between, he pleaded with whatever higher power there was, for tonight to be no different.

Maybe she would get a call from a friend and decide to go in a different direction. Her shift finished five minutes earlier. The lurker mentally traced her steps to this point. Two minutes at her pace — unless she worked overtime or someone gave her a lift.

They rarely did though.

He took a deep breath.

"Don't mess this up," he thought, unsure whether the words were to himself or to her – by changing her plans and deciding not to walk in his direction, despite spending the last two weeks passing the spot he now waited at.

It would be just like her to mess up his planning. Just like all of them. Then came the clicking of her heels, and the smell of perfume confirming it was her; the scent of apple which prompted him to lick his lips. Or perhaps it was the anticipation of what he was about to do. None of the food she ever gave him made him feel this way.

Patience, he told himself as his feet seemed to develop a mind of their own, tugging at his legs in an attempt to cut her off.

One second!. His legs readied themselves. *NOW.*

He sprang out of his hiding place — darting after her until she turned around. He toyed with her for a while, allowing her to think she might have a chance at escape. The real fear showed in her eyes when he grabbed her arms, pinning them to her sides. He smiled when he saw her long red hair. It almost looked like a flame underneath the streetlamp. He was about to extinguish that fire.

She recognised the familiar face. Her body went rigid as he reached into his jacket and pulled out the knife, reminding him of the time he had to pretend to be a *plank in the school play. She would have made a good plank, but that wouldn't be her role tonight.* He had gone over the plan in his mind. The victim struggled, unsuccessfully of course, but it was fun. His mind was already skipping ahead to the outcome.

"What are you...?" she began — bringing him back to reality, which wasn't playing out like he imagined it would. Something needed to be done to get things back on track. This was a moment to savour, not rush.

He kept his hands on her arms and tilted his head to kiss her lips. Her breath was minty; the source of the mint flavour (her chewing gum) was still in her mouth. He rolled it onto his tongue, then removed his hand from her right arm so he could take the gum and pocket it. He wanted a souvenir. That would be better than nothing.

She screamed, forcing him to clamp her mouth shut with his hand. Even the pain of teeth mauling at his hand wasn't enough to deter him. The struggle had begun.

Chapter One

I never imagined my own death. Why would I? I was thirty-six years old. I had years left, or so I thought. I changed my mind about that when I woke up in the morgue. The dead body…my dead body laid out in front of me, provided a good indication that I no longer needed to draw breath. My eyes were open, and I could almost imagine I was staring at myself. Yet I struggled to look away from the shell I used to inhabit. My eyes wandered from my bruised face to the red mark on my neck, as if I was punched and strangled.

I closed my eyes. Maybe this would be gone when I opened them again. I'd have a laugh at the weird dream I had about being beside myself in the morgue. A brief memory popped into my head, hands gripping my arms, then the image faded. I opened my eyes to find my corpse wasn't gone though. It seemed to be taunting me for thinking I could make it not real.

"Did somebody do this to me?" I asked my dead self, only to receive no response. She just laid still. I wondered if all dead people looked like…well…like they had been scared to death I suppose.

I watched enough crime shows to recognise the signs of a murder. I recalled those same crime shows. Copying what they did seemed like my best option. The first step was to examine the victim. I took a deep breath, although no air went in or out of my body, but the action remained the same. I twisted my head from side to side. I stretched my arms like someone preparing for a boxing match or an intense workout session might do. It helped to imagine I was looking for clues about what happened to a fictitious character. If I stopped to dwell on the reality of my death, I might have panicked. It also helped to have no recollection of the circumstances leading up to my death. I remembered my family and Paul.

"Paul," I heard myself say. I felt a warm and familiar smile appear on my face, the same smile that formed on my lips whenever I thought of him. It faded a second later. Would I ever see him again? How would he learn where I was or what happened to me? Would he be upset? Okay, that last question seemed like a stupid one.

He was bound to be upset. I imagined the state I'd be in if the situation was reversed. Devastated didn't cover it.

A small rumbling sound jolted me out of my thoughts. It couldn't be my stomach. Ghosts don't get hungry. I looked at the wall as a silver lift door materialised out of the brickwork. I took another glance at my body, only then did I become aware of the slash starting at my right breast and ending at my stomach. Someone had cut me; I really was murdered. I knew I wasn't suicidal — but even if I had been — I ruled out the chances being able to cut myself open that much without passing out before I finished.

The lift pinged and the door opened. I walked no more than ten steps, only stopping to glance back at my remains when I was standing next to the open lift. My corpse looked much further away than it should have been.

I don't remember stepping inside, but I found myself in the lift. Some people might have chosen to step back out, but the buttons caught my attention. Instead of the usual ground floor, first floor etc; one arrow pointed up and another pointed down. I tried them both, but nothing happened. Then I spotted a circle. It was lit up and I hesitated before pressing it.

I closed my eyes as light flooded the small space. The doors clicked shut, then jerked forward, instead of moving up or down.

When I looked again, I was stood at the gates of my old primary school. I always believed the gates of Heaven would resemble those gates. They were big and golden, almost shining in the sunlight. I was shorter. I could tell I had shrunk in height by how much closer to the ground I was.

"Ouch," I yelped in a much younger voice as someone pulled my hair and ran off. I realised I was around the age of seven again. I remembered the scene as I yelled, "Paul."

Chasing after the boy brought back memories of how this ended. I tried to get my legs to stop running, but I had no control over my younger body while I chased the seven-year-old version of Paul around the playground.

My mum arrived to collect me, like the first time this happened.

"Why does Paul always pull my hair?" I asked, despite remembering my mother's answer.

"Maybe he likes you," she suggested.

"Boys are weird," I announced.

"Sarah, you're so smart. It took me twenty-five years to figure that out," my mum joked.

Without warning, my surroundings disintegrated, then reformed around me. I remembered the new scene. It was the following day. I ran up to Paul before school started, and handed over half of my chocolate bar.

"My mum says you like me. That's okay," I told him. "I like you too." I leant forward and kissed his cheek.

"Urgh, gross!" he exclaimed, rubbing at his entire face as though it would spread. "I don't like you," he yelled, then scurried away. A teacher found me sobbing on the playground tarmac when I was supposed to be in class.

The playground evaporated, and I was in the lift again, moving backwards this time. The door opened. I found myself outside a morgue and at the right height again. The lift vanished, but the people walking and driving past didn't react as though they had seen anything unusual. That's when I spotted him heading towards me. If my heart still worked, it would have sped up.

"Paul," I cried out as he walked away from the morgue. "Paul!"

This was the Paul of the present day. As I caught up with him in the nearby carpark, I noticed he looked tired and his eyes were red from crying, I found myself hoping those tears were over me.

"Please," I begged, "you have to be able to see me or least sense that I'm here." All our years together should mean we shared a connection which would tell him I was still around. How could he not sense me? I reached out to touch his arm, my hand passing through without so much as a shudder from him. "Please," I whispered.

"Hi," he said, although it sounded more like a sigh and he didn't sound happy or surprised.

"Oh, thank God," I gasped, not caring about his lack of enthusiasm. I'd snap at him later. For the moment, it was enough for me that he realised I was still with him. I knew we had a strong connection. There was no reason he shouldn't pick up on my spirit still hanging around.

"Is she inside?" I heard my mother's voice from behind me.

It struck me, Paul was talking to her, not me. I wanted to cry, except it turned out I couldn't do that anymore either.

"Yes, but you shouldn't go in. She's not how you remember…" Paul began.

"I want to see her, I admit it's been a while because…never mind. She's still my daughter," my mother insisted, dabbing her eyes.

I leaned closer to check for any actual tears. It wouldn't be the first time she pretended to cry.

I felt a pull, taking me to somewhere else, but tried to stand my ground.

"No," I demanded. "I need to know," but the magnetism was too strong, yanking me away from the street into what felt like nothingness.

I became trapped in darkness, maybe for days. Time spread out like the dreams I used to have of endless corridors that went on and on, never leading anywhere. I had to close my eyes because my mind started playing tricks on me, making me believe I saw movement in the dark. At first it was just shadows, then my eyes created the visible outline of a woman, curvy with long hair and someone else. I couldn't make out who either of them were or determine the gender of the second person. I only knew that I didn't want to watch, because something bad was about to happen to the woman.

When I dared to open my eyes the darkness lingered, but I knew I was in my bedroom. I could just make out Paul lying there in the middle of the bed we used to share. It reminded me of the times I used to get up and read books on my tablet as he slept. Occasionally, I'd glance up from the vintage reading chair and perceive his outline asleep on the bed.

My comfort at seeing the familiar sight quickly turned to annoyance at him for taking over my side of the bed. I didn't need sleep anymore. His actions still seemed so careless. Shouldn't he be putting my favourite item of clothing over a pillow and falling asleep with his arms around it, maybe while crying? I didn't want him to suffer. It didn't seem like he had just lost his fiancée though. I took a step forward to have a closer inspection. Although his eyes stayed shut, I guessed he was awake. I could always tell. He spent all his time thinking, except when he slept. That's the only time he ever looked peaceful. I saw that he appeared to be far from peaceful so close-up. His eyes twitched, and his mouth hung open as if he wanted to call out for help. Maybe he was asleep after all. He was having a nightmare, but I experienced a twinge of relief.

"Paul." I knelt by the bed and whispered his name.

He didn't hear me. As my eyes adjusted, I noticed the damp on his cheeks. I felt a rush of guilt over my earlier thoughts and longed to wipe his tears away, then soothe him by rubbing his back the way he used to like.

"How long have I been gone?" I asked.

Again, no answer. Even before I spoke, I understood that my words were wasted on him. I needed to listen to my own voice, if only to confirm I was still there, even if I wasn't all there.

"That's it," I thought out loud. "I'm just crazy and I'm in a psychiatric ward."

Although, I knew deep down that as crazy as everything seemed, it was all real.

"Paul," I said again. I cried without actual tears once more, which made me feel worse and like I had turned into my mother. "I don't understand why this happened. None of this makes sense."

I reached out my hand to touch his face, but he didn't react. Could he really feel nothing when my hand passed through into his jaw? I snatched my hand back, freaked out by the unnatural sight. Horror movies never struck a chord with me. Crime drama maybe, but not make-believe monsters or ghosts. Of course, I understood by that point, ghosts do exist. Monsters, I'm not so sure about, other than the human variety.

I had no sense of time to determine how long I stayed crouched by the side of the bed, before the familiar droning of the alarm broke the silence. I never understood how anyone ever believed the awful noise might be a good way to start their day.

Paul dragged himself out of bed to get on with his day. I always told him he worked too hard. He was the type of guy who would wheel himself into work with two broken legs unless somebody stopped him. Who would stop him from pushing himself too hard now?

"Now is not the time to be strong," I called out after him as he went into the bathroom. I admit I was a bit riled at him for going into work at a time like this. I mean, I died. Didn't that grant him some time off? I assumed it to be his way of coping, by trying to get things back to normal.

Ten minutes later he left for work.

"Bye then," I called out as he ambled out of the door. By now I'd given up on him ever seeing or hearing me, but it presented itself as a better alternative to saying nothing.

I wondered if I should go after him. If not, what should I do all day while he was at work?

I thought of my mum and sister. I hadn't seen my mum since that night outside the morgue, however long ago that was. I couldn't even remember the last time I'd seen my sister, or my final words to her. I decided to check in on my mother.

Chapter Two

I began to get the hang of how to travel from one place to another. A few moments of closing my eyes and concentrating on where I wanted to be, worked most of the time. I appeared outside my mum's house in Stretford, as two policemen walked up the small pavestone pathway and returned to their car. I figured they needed to question potential witnesses, but I doubted my mum was there at the time of my murder. So, she wouldn't have been able to help. I went inside and listened to the hushed conversation between my mum and my sister.

Emma's perfectly manicured nails dug into the oak table where her hand rested as she propped herself against it.

"It's just procedure I'm sure," my mum said, before changing the subject. "Cup of tea? And can you stop sitting on the table please?"

"I don't think a cup of tea will fix things this time," Emma snapped. "Tea won't bring Sarah back, will it?

And I wasn't sitting; I was leaning." Her voice broke and I recognised she was close to tears. She took a step away from the table.

I thought you didn't care; my thought came from nowhere.

I watched as my mum pulled her closer into a hug. I wished I could hug them both and tell them I hadn't gone anywhere. Again, part of me resented them for not sensing my spirit. I expected Paul to sense I was still around, but he hadn't. Mum and Emma were my blood though. That had to count for something, but clearly not.

"I'm here," I said, as my cheeks flooded with tears. I thought I was no longer capable of producing them. I lifted my hand to wipe them away, but they weren't even real tears, just imagined. My face felt like it should be damp, but it wasn't. I assumed it resembled the experience of someone who loses an arm or a leg, but imagines pain where the missing limb used to be.

Phantom tear syndrome, I decided. Typical. I spent my whole life being strong and never crying, except under extreme circumstances; now I wanted to cry over my early death and I couldn't.

"I don't want to be here anymore," I said.

I closed my eyes and allowed myself to be swallowed by the darkness again.

"Are you ready?" a voice asked from somewhere in the empty space I called The Nothingness.

"Are you talking to me?" I asked.

"Do you see anybody else?"

"No, but I can't even see you," I replied.

"I'm sorry about that."

There was a sound like a switch. Followed by a buzzing. A light came on from above. Despite looking up, I couldn't establish its source. I guessed the person responsible for the light didn't have to pay an energy bill.

The walls were white, and there was no sign of the owner of the voice. The lift materialised again, near enough for me to see both buttons lit up inside. I'd had time to reflect on events since discovering my own body in the morgue. Questions were starting to form in my mind. Did someone intend for me to pick one? Up or down? Instructions would have been helpful. It wasn't too much to ask. Normal lifts have a notice informing you what to do in case of an emergency. Why shouldn't this lift? Waking up in a morgue next to your own corpse, then stepping into a lift that appears out of nowhere and being given a choice of up or down, felt like as much of an emergency than any other. I shouldn't be the one to make that choice. It seemed obvious that I would choose up. Nobody would want to go down.

"No," I called out. "I can't go, not yet."

It couldn't be that simple and I still wanted to find out who killed me.

"But you said you didn't want to stay," the voice reminded me, imitating surround sound coming through the walls.

My eyes managed to make out his form but the light from above us became too bright for me to see his features. He seemed to be a person though, with two arms and legs. A little tall maybe – but not freakishly so.

"Yes," I admitted, "but I'm not ready to leave either. I can't leave my family and Paul. And I don't know what happened. How did I die?"

"Okay," he said. With that one word he vanished, taking the light with him.

I was bathed in darkness for a few seconds, before I found myself back at my mum's house.

"Hey, come back. I need answers," I yelled.

Silence.

"Hello!" I ran past my mum and her cup of tea, through the closed door and outside into the street, but there was no sign of him. "Get back here you...." I began

"Hey, keep the noise down, you're giving me a headache," a man who had just walked past said as he turned to glare at me. His eyes were bloodshot, and his hair looked like it had never met a comb.

"You can see me?" I looked around to make sure he wasn't talking to anyone else.

"Of course I can see you. I can bloody hear you too. Keep it down, please. I've got a hangover." He rubbed the front of his head.

"Oh my god; you can see me," I gasped

"Oh no. You're one of them, aren't you?" The man looked around at the rest of the street, then back at me. "Fine," he relented. "I can see you. Follow me if you must, but don't talk. I refuse to stand around here looking like a lunatic who's talking to himself."

I followed him to his house across the street in silence, which was more difficult than I expected.

"What do you want?" he demanded after shutting the door.

I couldn't resist looking around at the interior of the house. Because of the open plan setup downstairs, I saw straight into the lounge area and the kitchen beyond it. Even from that distance it was obvious he wasn't exactly house-proud. My sense of smell died with me, but my mind filled in the blanks — making me gag at the thought of excessive dust, stale unwashed dishes and mould-ridden food from the overflowing bin. I reminded myself I wasn't there for a Better Homes photo shoot though.

"What do you mean?" I asked, not commenting on the domestic disaster all around me. It wasn't easy, but being dead and unable to catch anything helped. If I was alive, I would have gotten out of there and had a week of continuous showers, possibly scrubbing off my skin and ending up bleeding to death. Death by excessive scrubbing, or murder; which was worse?

"Well, you people always want something."

"You people?" I questioned, wondering if he was ghost-ist, if that was even a real term.

"I mean ghosts, dead people or whatever. You realise you're dead, right?"

"No shit, Sherlock." The only reason I followed him home was the hope of a two-sided conversation and some help getting answers, not for him to point out the obvious.

"Fine. If you don't want my help, sod off." He pointed towards the door as if that was my only way out.

"I'm sorry," I forced out the words. "I haven't been social for a while. Maybe it's because I keep talking to people and they won't talk back, because they can't hear me."

"Well, I don't have that luxury. So, what do you want?"

"I need to find out what happened to me."

"You don't remember how you died?"

"No, it's all a blank. The police went to my mum's house. Maybe I was murdered," I suggested, not wanting to think of the possibilities. Though the image of the hands gripping my arms, replayed in my head. The image might be anything: Something I watched on television, someone who wanted to hurt me, or Paul being affectionate. The feeling behind it made me feel anything but affectionate. I sensed a hint of recognition and fear as if someone I knew was trying to hurt me.

"The memory loss happens for a reason. Whatever you learn, you might wish you hadn't."

"I want to know," I insisted. How could I pass on or whatever I was meant to do, while conscious of the fact that the person responsible for ending my life might not be a stranger?

"Alright then, what's your name?" he asked. "I'll look into it, see if I can find out anything."

"Sarah," I told him. "Sarah Winters. Thank you, for anything you can find."

I returned home in the evening. I still called the house in Salford Quays my home, even though I suppose it wasn't anymore. The fact that Paul was starting to go through my belongings and pack them up, confirmed how things would never go back to the way they had been before. There was no chance of me getting back in my body and not being dead anymore. I needed to accept that, but moving on seemed like an impossibility without closure.

"I wish you were here," Paul said to the stuffed bear he'd bought me on my last birthday, but I figured he meant me and not the bear.

"But I am here," I replied.

He carried on packing until he picked up a photograph of us together at my fifteenth birthday party.

I'd avoided him since the playground incident, but my mum let me invite the whole class. He was in my class that year. Paul surprised me when he turned up. I assumed he hated me, but it turned out he'd grown up since then. We spent most of my party talking. My mum intervened for the final hour and made sure I talked to some of my other guests, who in her words, "came here to celebrate your birthday, young lady".

Other than talking to Paul, the party was lame with eighties music and a caterpillar cake which would have been more suited to a seven-year-old. It tasted good though; chocolate and sugary goodness. I rested my hand over my stomach, wishing I could eat cake, or anything else. I took food for granted, the smell, the taste and that satisfied feeling at the end of the meal. Paul understood all of that. It's why he became a chef.

I smiled at my memories while I watched Paul in the present moment. He was trying so hard to carry on. I saw it in his eyes, but he never liked to give up. This was no exception. He lay down on the bed, keeping to one side this time, as if he expected me to come back and join him at any moment. I wished I could, to tell him it had all being a mistake. I wasn't dead; everything was going to be all right, but those were all lies. Even if I lied to Paul, he wouldn't be able to hear me anyway.

People who have lost a loved one always have different stories about their grief and how hard the loss is for them, but nobody ever mentions how difficult it is for their loved one — to watch everyone else getting on with their lives, or grieving. Which is worse? I still can't say.

I hovered above the side of the bed which used to be mine, then turned my head to look at Paul while he drifted off to sleep.

"I miss you," I murmured as I closed my eyes.

"I miss you too," he said.

My eyes shot open. It took all my self-control not to shriek that he heard me. If he really could hear me, I didn't want to freak him out by shouting in his face.

"Paul," I allowed myself to say, hoping I hadn't imagined it

He sprang up and switched on the bedside lamp, looking all around the room, including under the bed and in the wardrobe

"Seriously?" I demanded. "Why would I be in the wardrobe?"

It didn't matter though because he couldn't hear me anymore. His eyes stared past me, then he walked through me on his way to the bathroom.

***

"He heard me!" I said, as I appeared in front of the one person able to see me.

"Yes, I'm fine thanks. How are you? Please come in."

Steve sat on the sofa, staring at the television even though it was on standby.

"I'm sorry." Had I left my manners somewhere in the afterlife, or did I never have them to start with? "I don't even know your name."

"You're not interested in knowing my name." he told me.

"Yes I am," I argued.

"No, you're not."

"Come on," I told him. "It can't be that bad. What is it? Edmund? Lucio?"

"No."

"Worse?" I teased. "Dracula?"

"You're being silly now," he said, trying not to smile. "You seriously want to know my name?"

"Yes!" I exclaimed.

'It's Steve.'

"Oh, well that's boring. Why didn't you want to tell me?"

"They…the ghosts never ask," he replied.

"It's nice to meet you, Steve. I'd shake your hand but…"

"Yeah, sorry." He looked away. "I can't help with that. Anyway, who heard you?"

"What?"

"When you burst into my flat without knocking…or banging your chains or whatever; you were yelling that someone heard you."

"Oh yeah, Paul." I couldn't believe I'd forgotten. "I was hovering next to Paul. He was asleep, or almost asleep. I said something to him, then he replied." I stopped for a breath, even though I didn't need to breathe anymore. The routine of taking in air must have remained imprinted in my mind.

"And you're sure he heard you? He wasn't talking in his sleep?"

"I'm sure," I insisted.

"Okay," Steve responded. "It can happen sometimes. When the brain is relaxed, it's more open to sounds it wouldn't pick up on while in a more focussed state of mind. If he was falling asleep, that would explain it."

"So, I can talk to him? To anyone, if they're falling asleep?"

"Falling asleep or in a relaxed state, sometimes," Steve said.

I looked at him and saw that he was reading from the open book he held. I also noticed the numerous shelves of books about ghosts and the afterlife on two large bookcases made of cheap plastic. The bookcases and the books they contained may have been the only area in Steve's house that he ever gave attention to when it came to cleaning. There wasn't a speck of dust on them. He valued his books, if nothing else.

"You're like an expert on this stuff," I realised out loud.

"When you see your first ghost at primary school, then go home and tell your parents, only for them to act like you're making it up, you realise you can't talk to anyone about it. You have to find things out for yourself."

"That sounds awful," I said, paying close attention to Steve's appearance. He was could use a shave and seemed a little gaunt. His light brown hair still lacked that first meeting with a comb, and his eyes looked weary. From the look of his plain black jeans and creased grey t-shirt, complete with various food stains, it had been a few days since he'd changed clothes or even had a wash. He could be attractive if he put in the effort though.

"I dealt with it." He shrugged

"How do you deal with something like that?" I asked.

"I discovered that if I was off my face, I could block them all out. I got halfway through studying for my journalism degree while I was high. That's better than I'd have done without the drugs, with them bothering me all the time."

I understood he meant ghosts like me, but I chose not to take offence.

"Why did you drop out?" I asked, picking up on the part where he got halfway through his studies.

"You don't want to hear this."

"I show up here in your…home," I began as I glanced around at the chaos, "demanding that you help me, even though I don't know you. The least I can do is learn a little about you. I mean I've got time, I'm not getting any older." I smiled, then gave him what I hoped was a defiant expression as I waited for him to respond. The fact that I'd waited so long to ask about his life caused me to wonder if I had always been so selfish, or if it was a side effect of being dead.

"One night before an important exam, the drugs stopped working and this woman, I mean the ghost of a woman. She wouldn't leave me alone. I took more pills, to help me study in peace."

"You overdosed?" I guessed.

"It wasn't intentional. I wanted to study for the exam, but after that I dropped out. I became the freak who tried to kill himself. What could I say? I did it to block out the ghosts?"

"I see how that would have made everything worse, sorry," I said, wishing I had solid arms to hug him with. He reminded me of an abandoned puppy in a pound that nobody wanted, because all the other puppies were cuter and better house trained. I regretted trying to drag him into my problems. "I never thought what it must be like. I can go.".

Disappointment hit me, but I intended to leave if he wanted me to.

"No," he protested. "I mean, you're okay for a ghost. Besides, I have something to tell you."

"What?" I asked.

"You were right. It wasn't an accident, someone killed you. At least that's what the police report says."

I suspected my death was a murder, but had to ask, "who would want to kill me?"

"I can't imagine," he replied, going back to his sarcastic self. "You're such pleasant company when you're not walking into people's homes and demanding help."

Chapter Three

Instead of going back to Paul's place, I spent the night at Steve's — looking over newspaper websites and clippings he'd collected from articles reporting on my murder.

They hadn't found the killer or a motive yet, unless they were keeping it a secret from the press. Some journalists seemed to take pleasure in writing about my death. The word "mysterious" was thrown around a lot. All the major newspapers clambered for an exclusive, by offering rewards to anyone who contacted them with new information. They claimed they would pass this information onto the police. They omitted the part about using it to sell thousands more copies of their cheap publications, before handing over the info to the authorities as an afterthought.

"I'm sorry I couldn't be more help," Steve told me as the sun rose, shining through the faded blue curtains.

"Don't be," I replied. "At least you tried."

We didn't speak for a few minutes.

My mind seemed to be screaming at me to not give up, but what could I do?

"I'm a ghost," I exclaimed as an idea occurred to me.

"No shit, Sherlock," he repeated my earlier line back at me.

"No, I mean I can go anywhere, right? And people won't see me."

"Ah!" He began to follow my line of thought. "And you're considering making a visit to the police station? Maybe the evidence room?"

"Why didn't I think of this before?" I asked.

"Because you're missing something."

"What?"

"Evidence is usually kept in files inside drawers or in lockers, as in locked away. Here catch this," he said, as he threw a small rubber ball at me.

Without thinking, I tried to catch it, but the ball went straight through my hands and ricocheted against the wall and the chair a few times before rolling under the table and landing next to the pile of porn magazines. I kept up the charade that I hadn't noticed them.

"Crap." I grasped the point Steve was making. "I can't touch anything."

"But I like the way your mind works," he told me. "Have you checked out the men's changing room yet? Because I would totally be spending all my time in the ladies changing rooms if I was a ghost."

That revelation didn't surprise me. My head tilted towards the magazines. I looked at Steve, narrowing my eyes and scrunching up my face.

"You're lucky I can't touch anything, because if I could I'd be throwing things at your head right now."

"Hey," he protested. "That's no way to treat someone who can help you."

"How?" I questioned.

"Well, I'm not sure how you would go about it, but I've come across ghosts who can move things. I mean, they weren't exactly touching the objects at the time. If I had to guess, I'd say it was more of a mind-over-matter process using the energy around them."

"Like telekinesis?"

"Maybe."

"But you don't know how I can learn it?"

"I think it's a ghost thing and I'm not a ghost," he replied.

"I'll figure it out," I decided.

"How?"

Why did he have to be so full of questions instead of helping?

"I don't know, but I will." I stared at his TV and willed it to move.

"You're trying it now, aren't you?" Steve looked at me with a mixture of curiosity and concern, probably over the potential destruction of his television set.

"Yeah," I muttered, trying to concentrate. If I could produce sweat, it would have been dripping from my forehead. It reminded me of the time Paul took me to the gym with him. He said to stick to the smaller weights, but I saw a woman who looked like she had stepped out of a fitness video. She began lifting heavier weights than some of the men. If she could do it, why couldn't I? So, I ignored Paul's warning much to his amusement. I never went back to the gym after that. I wouldn't be surprised if the staff still watch and laugh over the CCTV footage of my lame attempts to lift half my own body weight.

"I doubt it's going to be that easy, but just in case, can you not practice it on my forty-two-inch plasma TV?" Steve requested.

"Sorry." I said, stopping. "I'd be lucky to move a fly anyway. Your forty-two-inch plasma is safe." At least there was no camera recording me this time, and it's not like I could feel so embarrassed that I might die. That ship had already sailed.

Steve must have picked up on my disappointment, He looked around the room.

"Something smaller maybe? Like a pencil." He rested one on the palm of his hand. "Make this float out of my hand."

The idea was a desperate one, but I felt ready to try desperate. I tried to push it with my mind; I tried imagining the pencil floating. Each time, it showed an unusual amount of stubbornness for an inanimate object, by refusing to budge. I lifted my hand in the direction of the pencil. I waved one hand around, then both. I pointed my finger, then I even yelled random words like "shazam" and "elevate" but nothing worked.

Steve looked at me, his mouth twitching as he struggled to keep a straight face.

"It's not funny," I snapped.

That made him worse and he erupted into laughter the way someone might if they hadn't laughed in a long time, but finally found something to amuse them. It was loud; his body shook until tears streamed down his eyes.

"Well, I'm glad this amuses you at least."

"Oh, come on," Steve teased. "You should have seen yourself."

I tried not to smile but Steve's amusement was infectious. Before I could stop myself, we were both laughing at the ridiculousness of my failed efforts to move the pencil.

"Can I come back later?" I asked. "I'll knock, or I'll stand outside your door and yell knock knock. That might be the best I can do."

"Sure, are you going already?"

"Steve, I've been here all night."

As I concentrated on getting back to Paul, I heard Steve say, "the first time in years that I get a girl back to my place and she's a ghost. Typical!"

***

I found Paul working at The Crusty Edge. He was always a great cook. I was just the waitress. I could barely boil an egg without ruining it. I liked to bake though, and I was good with people. At least I had been when I was alive. Now I wasn't so sure. Most of my conversations, with the exception of Steve, were one-sided since my death. Waiting tables and chatting with the customers seemed like somebody else's life.

Paul began berating one of the younger cooks, which wasn't like him. The poor guy who I didn't recognise, looked like he was close to tears.

"I'm sorry," he told Paul. "I only turned away for a minute to check the beef and when I came back the potatoes had boiled over. I'll clean up the mess."

"If you can't do your job right, there are plenty of other people who can," Paul threatened.

"Please, I need this job," he pleaded.

Paul waved him off in the same way someone might try to deter a fly on their food.

I guessed the man must have started recently. We had a higher staff turnaround over the summer months. That's when students look for work, trying out jobs until they find one they like, or hate less than other jobs they've tried.

"Go home. You won't be paid for today. When you come back tomorrow, I don't want any more mistakes from you," Paul snapped.

Anyone closer to Paul's age might argue over the legality of receiving no pay for the work he did before being sent home. The poor man looked flustered as he gathered his things. I doubted he would return the next day. Paul lacked the authority to send anyone home, but the new cook didn't realise that.

Paul turned to the rest of the kitchen staff and yelled, "somebody clean up this mess for Christ's sake."

They scurried around, grabbing cloths and a mop bucket.

"What is wrong with you?" I snapped — and as I did, a plate flew up from the counter and just missed Paul's head.

"Oh! I did that," I exclaimed I raised my arms in the air and spun around, laughing loudly. I only stopped spinning at the thought that I could have hurt Paul. My laughter halted and my smile faded. I examined the faces of Paul and the others in the kitchen.

Nobody seemed to be hurt and none of them looked impressed, but why would they? It wasn't like anyone could see or hear me.

"Who did…" Paul began, looking around as if expecting to catch someone close enough to have thrown or knocked the plate. His perplexed expression told me he knew that nobody could have. "Okay," he said, regaining his composure, "somebody clean this up as well."

A waitress I recognised, called Shelly, grabbed a dustpan and brush to sweep up the fragments, even though she had only entered the kitchen to hand over a food order.

I walked through the door and out of the dining area. I recognised an elderly couple as they entered the restaurant. I used to chat to them all the time. The woman's name was Martha, I think. I used to know her husband's name too, but death caused me to become forgetful at times. Even though I understood they wouldn't be able to hear or see me, I went over to their table.

"Excuse me, young man," Martha called out to the man who Paul reprimanded earlier.

He turned around, mid-dash to the door to retreat home, forcing his best smile in their direction. His face remained red.

"Could we see a menu?" Martha asked.

"Of course, I'll just get the waitress," he said.

"Not the short redhead, we're in a rush today and don't have time for her constant yammering," the old man spoke up.

"Yammering?" I demanded.

The cook looked at them. His mouth hung open, but no words came out. His face was flushed again. I worried he might pass out from all the stress that his body seemed ill-equipped to handle. His hands dived into his pockets, despite the training we all received telling us never to put our hands in our pockets. It looks so unprofessional.

Martha said, "you seem lost for words. Is everything alright?"

"Just..." he looked around. I'm guessing to check that Paul was out of earshot. "We only had one petite redhead work here. Before my time. I've seen photos of her, but I don't feel comfortable bad-mouthing the dead. My grandmother had superstitions about the whole..."

"Good lord," Martha gasped, "the red-haired waitress died? Oh, we didn't hear about that. She was such a lovely woman, wasn't she, Philip?"

"Oh yes, ever so bubbly and friendly," he said, looking at his wife and nodding like his head was out of control.

I decided I had listened to enough of their insincerity. I always tried to be friendly to them both when they ate at the restaurant. Why would they want to be served by someone else? I wished I could be alive for thirty seconds just to be able to serve them, by dropping the contents of the milk jug all over their expensive clothes, paid for with all the money they saved by never tipping me for my excessive hard work.

I went to find Paul again. He was outside in the car park. I watched as he sat down on the wall, then lit a cigarette.

"When did you start smoking?" I asked at the same time as a familiar voice behind me. I turned around to face Emma.

Although she was two years younger than me, I recognised my features in her face; the same cheekbones and thin lips. She modelled sleek black hair while I was a frizzy red-head, but we looked similar. I mean what I used to look like. I had no idea what I looked like as a ghost. I didn't show up in the mirror anymore.

"Since the stress of all of this," Paul retorted, his voice full of accusation.

"Don't talk to her like that," I snapped.

"I lost her too, she was my sister. Do you think I wanted this?"

"You didn't say anything about her that night, did you?" Paul demanded.

"Neither did you," Emma accused.

"Why are you here?" Paul asked

"I came to see if you're okay. I haven't seen you since…"

"So, you came back for seconds?" Paul asked. The words dripped with bitterness.

I wasn't used to seeing this side of him.

"No, I…" she began.

He lunged towards Emma. For a moment I thought he might headbutt her, but he kissed her instead. His lips pressed hard against hers for a moment before he pulled away.

"Is that what you want?"

"No." Emma took a step back, but he grabbed her arms and pulled her closer, then kissed her again until she stopped struggling and became more involved in the kiss. She allowed her tongue to slip into his mouth and clung to him as if she was on a sinking ship and he was the last lifeboat.

"Get off her," I yelled.

My first reaction was to grab Paul to drag him away. I didn't stop to remind myself about my lack of a physical body. My arms passed through him and I had to watch until I heard him mutter, "Sarah."

Emma pulled herself away saying, "I won't be her." She stepped back. "You know I would do anything for you, but not like this." She turned and left.

Paul watched her go, took a step, then stopped before glancing back at the restaurant.

"Don't you dare go after her," I warned,

Relief washed over me when Paul didn't try to stop her, but walked back inside instead.

My mind struggled to get around what I had just witnessed. Did my sister and Paul have something to do with my death? Were they seeing each other behind my back? Emma never made a secret of the fact she found Paul attractive, but I'd trusted her. I thought Paul loved me and would never do anything to hurt me. I trusted him too. How could I have been so wrong?

My head was flooded with images. Me and Paul dating when I was fifteen, going to McDonald's for our first date because it was all either of us could afford. Then Emma telling me that she had started seeing Paul while I was studying Journalism at Sunderland University. Paul insisted that we should see other people, the conversation came back to me.

"I love you," I'd told him.

"I love you too. I think you're better going to university and not having me holding you back though."

"You're not holding me back."

"Things happen at University. People change; they work out what they want or don't want."

Paul thought I might decide I didn't want him. I tried to persuade him that I would never do that, but his mind seemed made up.

Maybe he wanted to be with Emma and that's why he split up with me before I left Manchester. I recalled us getting back together after I graduated though. Emma tired of him, as she often did with her men. I lost count of the number of relationships she had after that. It became a running joke every time she announced she met someone special.

Judging by the way Emma kissed my fiancé, she never got over him and it seemed like they kept something going alongside my relationship with Paul.

I thought about trying to move the nearby skip to slam it into Paul next time he went outside for a smoke, but my surroundings evaporated around me and I found myself in the darkness again.

Chapter Four

I could see the faint outline of a wall at either side of me and heard the sound of rats scuttling around nearby as my vision adjusted, which led me to assume I was in an alley somewhere. That explained the limited amount of light. I jumped at the sound of footsteps before the figure of a long-haired woman raced past me while my eyes took in clearer images of my surroundings. Her breath sounded like an untrained runner on the last mile of a marathon with only one person behind her, neither wanting to be last. A few seconds later, another person rushed past, a man. His footsteps were louder and his breathing deeper, although less panicked than the woman's.

"Fucking bitch," he muttered.

I felt like I had heard the voice before — probably when the speaker hadn't been so out of breath.

"Please," she said.

My focus improved further, and I was able to see that we were standing at the back of a building which loomed over us, as if working with the man to conceal what he was about to do. The woman hit her fists against the back door, but he grabbed her by the hair. I spotted a glint of metal and guessed it came from a knife.

"No, no," she begged.

"You asked for this. You deserve this," he hissed into her ear. I noticed the glint again as he reached his hand around her throat.

There was screaming, mine, hers? I'm not sure. Maybe both of us were screaming. I closed my eyes, the same way I would if I was watching a horror movie.

"Sarah, Sarah," a familiar voice called my name.

I opened my eyes and found myself in Steve's house. The noodles on his fork had dropped off onto the coffee table, sending splatters of noodle juice onto the glass as if to frame them.

"What? I…"

"You just appeared here, screaming when I was eating my tea," he said, making the previous scene seem like it happened during some over-realistic nightmare.

"I was in an alley," I said, feeling like I might be crazy. It occurred to me that might be how ghosts turned into poltergeists. As I rolled the idea around in my head, I was sure I watched something similar on TV. I don't think the programme was a documentary, but they had to get their ideas from somewhere, right? Maybe the afterlife scrubbed away every trace of sanity over time. Was something like that happening to me?

When I caught Steve up on everything, he responded in his usual way.

"You've had a busy day."

I clenched and unclenched my fists, wondering if I could will my hand into physical form for just long enough to slap him. Why did he have to make light of the situation? I might have tried to throw his precious plasma TV across the room, but it weighed much more than the plate at the restaurant, and I hadn't meant to throw that.

"What does it mean?" I asked him.

"Sometimes memories get scrambled during the crossing over from life to death," he said.

His explanation made sense of the love triangle with Paul, Emma and myself. I wouldn't want to remember that and I'd be happy for the knowledge to become re-scrambled.

"I never witnessed someone murdered in an alley though. I know my memories are hazy, but I'm sure about that."

I was certain that wasn't a scrambled memory. The thing with Emma and Paul felt like it really happened as soon as I watched the replay in my head. The murder in the alley felt new, like I was seeing it or the first time.

"I have a theory about that," Steve said, reaching for one of his books.

He showed me a chapter about the ghosts of victims of violent crimes having a connection to their killers.

"That woman wasn't me though, it was dark, but her hair wasn't red like mine. It was deep brown, maybe. Or black."

"She might be his next victim," Steve suggested.

I didn't understand why I would be shown the next victim of my killer right after seeing Paul with Emma, unless he was the killer.

"Don't most killers know their victims?" I asked, wondering how connected to my killer I might be.

Steve picked up on my hint. "Why would Paul kill someone else after killing you?"

"I don't know. If he killed me to be with Emma, maybe he's going to kill someone else to get his way over something else." My theory sounded weak as I suggested it, but I recalled the hands against my arms, like Paul's hands against Emma's arms. Were they the same hands?

"I don't believe it's Paul," Steve said with a shrug.

My sister, with her jet-black hair could be the next victim, I thought, ignoring his doubt. The more I replayed the image in my head of the man chasing his victim, then slitting her throat — the more I envisioned both of their features. The man was Paul and his prey was my younger sister, the other woman I hadn't been aware of during my engagement. I still held onto the anger and disappointment I felt for Emma, but she was still my family. I shouldn't let her die because of that. I closed my eyes and thought of Paul.

When I appeared in his flat, I caught the last leg of an intense scene between him and Emma. She made panting sounds, with her eyes wide open and her mouth in an 'O' shape. He grunted, kissed her mouth as if he was going to eat it, then rolled off her. They hadn't wasted any time. If I was still alive, I might have thrown up.

I couldn't help questioning how after two people had just done that, later one of them might be capable of murdering the other. I'd had sex with Paul many times though. We were going to be married, or so I'd thought. However, we'd ended up with him killing me, so in that moment I reasoned that it wasn't so implausible.

What would the crime scene investigators do on the shows I used to watch? I asked myself the question. They would look for evidence, of course. I pushed my disgust to one side, at the sight of my fiancé and sister lying together, post-sex. I walked around the bedroom, grateful the bedside lamp was on to help me see, as I turned my back on Paul and Emma.

Make-up cluttered the surface on the chest of drawers, Emma's. She had made herself comfortable. The middle drawer was open, revealing a few of Paul's t-shirts on the left and her underwear on the right, black thongs and matching bras. He always liked it when I wore black lingerie, but those weren't mine. They were skimpier than anything I ever wore. My sister hadn't been on the pill long enough for her chest to expand much. I turned away; knowing that Emma almost had a whole drawer to herself wasn't helping me find evidence of Paul killing me. It would be hidden somewhere, not on display with the make-up and inappropriate underwear. I thought about the garage. When I was alive, Paul spent a lot of his free time in there. He claimed to be working on the second-hand car he bought at an auction. He used this as a reason to slope away at random intervals for over a year. I never had a reason to doubt him before. My knowledge of cars was limited, but it struck me as a long time to work on one car.

"I am so fucking gullible," I said, slamming my fist through the nearest wall. The ease of it passing through, without contact or any pain caused me to scream. Was there no way of venting my anger anymore?

I walked through the bedroom wall, no longer freaked out by the action. My mind was focussed on getting to the garage. I was prepared to walk through all the doors and walls I needed to in order to reach my destination.

I stood staring at the car, which resembled the same rust bucket I only saw a few times after Paul purchased it. It seemed obvious, even to me that he never worked on it. If anything, the car was in a worse state than the day he bought it. He deceived me, buying this thing, possibly as an alibi while he went out murdering women. I hadn't been the first. Had he been killing for the whole year, or longer and just decided he needed the car as a reason for his long disappearances? My mind flicked back to his old management job. His hours were random, and he often had to go in at short notice. The building was open twenty-four hours a day, so it didn't seem so far-fetched back then. When Paul was made redundant, he got the job at the restaurant. Disappearing at all hours would have looked suspicious. That's when he bought the car. I connected the dots and created a picture of my serial-killer fiancé.

I tried to focus as I continued to look around the garage. I searched the interior of the car, with my head inside the vehicle and the rest of me outside it. If Paul was able to see me and he decided to go to the garage, the sight would freak him out. The made me smile, until I spotted a red basque in the back seat. I couldn't pick the thing up, despite trying to levitate it with my mind, but it seemed small. It might fit a size six (or an eight at the most) but not me, a size ten. Paul knew my size and the only clothing he ever bought me were t-shirts on my birthday; the ones with stupid slogans on. I recalled one that said *Hot Stuff. Don't Touch*. I only ever wore it in winter, under a cardigan. He never bought me anything else wearable. The basque couldn't have been a surprise for me. I wouldn't have worn it if it was, even in my size.

I questioned whether the lingerie might be a trophy from one of his victims, aware that some killers like to keep something as a reminder. They also manage to come across as normal to their friends and family. It was possible that Paul had fooled me along with everyone else. Paul slept upstairs in the house, with my sister. The woman who kept something going with him while he was with me; my sister who had started a relationship with him when I went to university while I remained single, hoping we would get back together after I graduated. My sister, despite all of that. I shouldn't leave her to be murdered too.

I closed my eyes and transported myself back to Steve.

"You're back," his face creased, forming thin lines as though he was concerned. "I thought you might have done something stupid."

Figuring out Paul was definitely the killer didn't seem stupid to me, but I didn't want to waste time arguing.

"No, just investigating, and I found something. I need your help."

I explained to him about Emma and Paul being a couple now, and the basque I found in the car and all my thought processes in reaching the conclusion that Paul had been killing for years and keeping souvenirs of his victims. He listened to everything I said, until I felt talked out, then he responded.

"You say you only found one piece of physical evidence? It could be a present for Emma."

I flinched at the idea of Paul buying sexy underwear for Emma, not because he never bought it for me. I meant it when I said I wouldn't have worn it. Maybe that was my problem. Had I been too closed-minded? Is that why he had to cheat on me with my sluttier sister?

"I only looked in the bedroom a little and the garage," I stated. "I'm sure there's more, but one piece of evidence will do for now. I still need your help though."

"What do you want me to do?" Steve looked at me, his arms were crossed against his chest.

"Just go to the garage and get the basque out of the car. I can't get it myself. That's all," I tried to make my voice light, like I wasn't asking much from him.

"Oh, is that all? Just a bit of breaking and entering, with a dash of theft thrown in. A typical Tuesday night then."

"It's a Tuesday? That used to be my one definite day off," I said, realising I no longer had any concept of the days. Being dead meant no longer having to worry about shifts at work or appointments. However, I was concerned about the killer my sister was shacked up with.

"Focus," Steve said, waving his hand in front of my face. "What you're asking me to do could get me arrested, locked up in prison even. And do you have any idea how many people die in prison? That means ghosts of criminals haunting me. No thanks."

"But you can take the evidence to the police. Paul would get arrested and you would be saving countless lives," I reasoned.

I understood his reluctance. It can't be good to have ghosts haunting you because you're one of the few people who can see them. Criminal ghosts must be worse, but I needed help. He was the only person I had met with the ability to see ghosts.

"I'll make you a deal," I said. "You tell me someone else who has your gift and I'll get them to help me instead."

For a moment, I thought he looked disappointed.

"We don't all know each other. It's not like we hold an annual convention or something," he retorted.

"Then I'm sorry, but you're the only one who can help me."

Chapter Five

I stood outside the garage, wondering if Steve had changed his mind. My method of travel was faster than his, but he should have been there already.

"What took you so long?" I asked when he hurried across the residential road towards me. I heard the sound of a car driving away from the nearby side street. I assumed it was the taxi, and Steve hadn't wanted to be dropped off in view of the house.

"Only night buses run at this time of night and at random times that I'd need a degree in public transport to figure out. You owe me money for the taxi," he whispered, looking up at the bedroom windows.

"I don't carry cash. It would only fall through my ghost pockets," I retorted.

"Fine, let's get this done," he said, before walking around the outside of the house and reaching out to open the side door leading to the garage. It didn't open. He pulled at it again, then looked at me. The neighbours' security lights drew attention to the obvious annoyance on his face. "You didn't think to unlock the door," he hissed.

"I didn't need to," I replied, not having to lower my voice, because nobody else would hear me.

Steven opened his mouth to speak, but was interrupted by the creaking of the front door as it opened. I lifted my hand as a signal for him to be quiet. I recognised the sound. It could be mistaken for a car driver putting on the brakes too fast, to anyone who didn't know better.

"What?" he mouthed.

"Somebody's coming," I said, pointing in the direction of the front of the house. "This way," I instructed, leading Steve into the back garden, grateful someone had left the wooden gate was open.

I knew the person approaching us could only be my sister or Paul.

Steve's eyes followed my finger when I pointed at the fence leading to the next garden. He looked at it, then at me.

"Go, over the fence," I hissed. It was the sole means of escape for him.

He hesitated for a second. We both heard approaching footsteps, making a crunching sound over the gravel then something scraped against the ground. It only lasted a few seconds, stopping before either of us could identify the source. Steve turned and ran for the fence, scrambled over it and disappeared from my sight. I imagined him racing through adjoining gardens until he reached the last one. Then he would make his way home. The image in my head was not unlike the horse-races Paul would watch on our rare afternoons off work together.

I told him it was cruel to the horses to force them to leap over fences like that, with the weight of a person on their back. The chances of a fall were too high, and would result in the horse having to be put down.

'How would you like it if I sat on your back and made you leap over fences?' I asked.

He grinned and retorted, "Lose a few pounds and maybe I'll give it a go,"

I convinced myself he was joking. As a man, he couldn't understand how those words would affect a woman and make her feel self-conscious. He didn't mean to upset me.

I was snapped back to the present moment, by Paul standing in front of me with a shovel in his hands. The scraping sound must have been him picking it up. Would he have used it to kill Steve if he hadn't run off? Was he capable of that, or did he limit himself to killing women during their most defenceless moments?

Paul looked straight through me and at the fence. He took a step, then another, getting closer. I didn't know how far Steve had gotten. I couldn't let Paul spot him and give chase. I'm the one who persuaded Steve to attempt a break-in. It was my fault for not thinking about how he would get inside the garage. I had to stop Paul from going after him. I focussed on my emotions; my guilt over dragging Steve into this, my fear for his life, my resentment at Paul for deceiving me for so long and at myself for not realising anything was wrong. I stared at the shovel and felt surprised when Paul appeared to lose control of it. To anyone else, it would have looked like he flipped it around and smacked himself in the head with the flat side of the shovel.

"Yes," I exclaimed, as if I had just scored the winning goal in an important football match. I was never the sporty type when I was alive, but in that moment I could feel the victory sports-people must experience when achieving that all important goal, or after crossing the finish line of a marathon. Paul lay sprawled out on the grass, dazed and swearing.

I reminded myself of his secret activities as a killer; not like the man I fell in love with. That man was a character who Paul portrayed. He didn't exist any more than the cast of a film did, other than as actors who went back to their real lives when the filming finished. His real life consisted of murdering women.

I left Paul alone, knowing he was in no fit state to kill my sister or anyone else that night.

I arrived back at Steve's house before he did. I stood in front of one of the bookcases, reading the titles when he ran into the house, panting and locking the door behind him.

Key, dead lock, chain, a second key.

"I am so sorry," I said.

He stumbled backwards, grabbing at the wall, then a bookcase, before steadying himself on the banister at the bottom of the stairs.

"For what? Scaring the shit out of me just now, or outside Paul's garage earlier?" he asked.

"Both, I suppose. But I made sure Paul wouldn't follow you."

"What did you do?" he asked. His expression grew more serious and concerned than scared.

I couldn't help noticing him glance around, almost as if expecting Paul's ghost to appear and demand his help.

"Relax, I didn't kill him. I hit him with a shovel, but only injured him. He's still alive."

He seemed surprised at that, then almost proud when I told him how I'd focussed my mind to move the shovel in Paul's hand.

"Maybe I can do the same on the garage door," I offered.

"There's no way I'm going back there," Steve stated.

I wanted to argue but couldn't bring myself to insist he went back. I put him through enough already — turning his life upside down since the moment I met him outside my mum's house. I considered using my newfound mind powers to remove the evidence myself. Moving a shovel to hit Paul was completely different to moving the basque all the way to the police station though. It would be difficult if not impossible; not to mention all the attention it might attract. I smiled to myself at the notion of the basque seeming to float to the police station by itself. Then how would I alert the police that it was evidence of Paul's murderous ways?

"I'm an idiot," I announced.

"No," Steve said. His one-word reply lacked conviction.

"I never considered how we would get the evidence to the police, or how we would let them know what it is."

I'm guessing you claiming you can see dead people wouldn't go down so well?"

"Not so much," he agreed.

I wondered if he ever tried to tell anyone in authority about his ability before. He still looked a little pale and shook up from our attempted burglary and almost getting caught. So, I didn't think it was a good time to ask.

"Sorry," I said. "I shouldn't have asked you to go back there."

I decided to go check on my mum. I heard Steve call out something as I closed my eyes and thought about my mum's house. I was unable to make out the words though. They were distorted, as if I was hearing them in a void while I was somewhere between places.

My mum's house looked different when I got there. There were boxes stacked around the furniture. I spotted my mum sitting on the armchair in the middle of them. She held her phone against her ear, as she barked orders at whoever was unfortunate enough to be on the other end. She was moving; I worked that much out from the boxes and the instructions over the phone to make sure the van arrived by eleven in the morning.

I didn't understand it. She loved that house. We all lived there together; me, Emma and Mum, and Dad before he passed away. The thought of Dad jolted me out of my thoughts about the house. Had he crossed over? I hadn't seen him since I died. I hadn't seen any ghosts. I would have to ask Steve about it later.

As my mum finished the call, I asked myself how I would know where she was moving to. I panicked that I might never be able to find her again. We weren't close when I was alive. I don't know when we started to drift apart. We didn't have problems when I was a child. Maybe the problems began after Dad died. Mum never allowed me to visit him in the hospital.

What I can only describe as an apparition appeared to the left of the boxes. I remained in my mum's house, but my mum of the present moment remained oblivious as the scene from my past played out.

"Why can't I visit Dad?" a younger version of myself demanded. The red cardigan, matching skirt and white blouse told me I must have been in secondary school by that point.

"He's very ill, darling." My mum made a sniffling noise while wiping her face.

"Then why can't I see him?" I asked again. "If he's ill…" I couldn't finish the sentence.

I was fourteen and aware of death, although I'd didn't know anyone who had died. My mum's logic made no sense. If my dad was seriously ill, why would she insist on preventing me from saying goodbye in case he didn't make it?

"The doctors won't allow it." She wiped her face again. I was too upset and angry to realise back then, she wasn't crying real tears at all.

It was years later when both Emma and I picked up on the fact that she would 'cry' whenever things didn't go her way.

"I hate you and if Dad dies it's your fault I didn't get to see him," the younger me snapped, before grabbing her school bag and storming out of the house.

I had pinpointed when the relationship with my mum started to deteriorate. I also saw what a horrible person I was. Fake tears or not, it must have been difficult for my mum to know she was losing her husband, the father of her children. As the scene disappeared, I turned to look at my mum in the present moment.

She finished her phone call, then sat in silence, staring at the boxes. She didn't cry, but her eyes seemed sad and her face looked much older. Mum always looked young for her age. The boys at my high school would make crude comments about her. Men around her own age must have found her attractive too. I don't remember her ever dating anyone after Dad though.

I glanced over at the clock and realised it was almost three in the morning.

It's been a busy day, especially for a dead person, I thought. I had the impression that the afterlife would involve more rest. I chose to go back to Steve's, not wanting to watch my mother looking so morose, and I didn't want to watch over Paul as he nursed his head injury while planning his next murder. I'd rather have my ankles and wrists chained together and be escorted down to hell.

I was surprised to find Steve still awake. He sat on the sofa staring at something on his laptop.

"Knock knock," I said, lowering my voice — not wanting to startle him again.

"There's been a murder," he announced, instead of greeting me with a hello.

"What?" I wondered why he seemed so keen to tell me.

"It's breaking news on the Manchester Evening News website. Someone discovered the body of a dark-haired woman down an alley in The Northern Quarter. Some people on Facebook are saying her throat was slit, but the police haven't released any more details yet."

"But Paul …" I begin.

"It happened around midnight when we were outside Pauls' house trying to break into the garage. It couldn't have been him. There's no way he made it into town, murdered someone and got back to Salford Quays in time for you to…" Steve trailed off, while holding an imaginary shovel in his right hand and swiping it through the air.

"Shit, I honestly thought I figured out the killer," I said. Guilt hit me over attacking him with a shovel. A queue of questions forced their way into my head. Why did he move on so fast? What about the lingerie in the garage and all the times he claimed to be working on the car? Where was he during those times? Was he genuinely not the killer, or could he be working in a murderous tag team?

"I need to go," I said.

"Where?" Steve asked

"To Paul's. Maybe he's not a killer, or maybe he just didn't kill tonight, but he's hiding something and I need to know what it is."

Steve looked like he was about to argue, but stifled a yawn as he opened his mouth.

"You must be tired. Get some sleep," I told him. "I promise I won't do anything stupid."

Chapter Six

I appeared back in Paul's bedroom. He lay sprawled out in bed with a flannel folded over his forehead. I felt a rush of relief at the sight of Emma lying next to him. Not that I wanted to see my sister in bed with the man I used to love, but at least she was alive and hadn't been the woman in my vision. Paul wasn't that woman's killer either. It posed the question, what else he could be hiding, if it wasn't murdering people?

Paul's eyes opened, his hand reached up and took the flannel off his forehead. He grimaced. I saw why, even though the only light in the room came from the outside street lamps, and the hallway light through the gap in the bedroom door. His face was swollen and bruised. I put a lot of force into that blow, probably because I didn't know if it would work, so I made it work too well. Control was something I hadn't yet grasped.

He dressed even though it's wasn't light yet.

"Wake up," I said, standing next to my sister — hoping she would be in a state of rest between awake and asleep. Her loud snoring signalled that she wasn't the slightest bit awake though.

Paul continued to dress as I persisted in calling out to Emma. She didn't wake as Paul put on his shoes. I realised I had to follow him, because I had no way of getting her to wake up and confront him about where he was going at that time of night. I reasoned with myself that it's not normal behaviour for someone who works a dayshift to sneak out of the house in the middle of the night. He had to be a killer after all. Maybe he didn't have anything to do with the other murder, or he could be meeting with his accomplice.

I followed him to a house about ten-minutes away on foot. He knocked at the door, and as a blonde woman answered, I wondered if Paul was into sleeping around with women rather than killing them. Her outfit left little to the imagination. Her silk dressing gown failed to cover anything below the top of her thighs. I had bigger t-shirts, including those bought by Paul. In fact, most of the t-shirts he bought for me were a size or two bigger than I needed. Black lace was on show as a mild wind shifted the woman's dressing gown. She didn't attempt to cover up, and he didn't look at all concerned about trying to make her wear clothing two sizes too big for her. I suppose it was just me he liked to make feel frumpy. The scantily clad slut just smiled, standing aside as Paul entered the house. I dived through the door as soon as it shut behind them.

I followed them down to a basement. Nothing could have prepared me for what I saw. The basement was full of whips and chains.

The woman released herself from the gown. It dropped to the concrete ground to reveal the lacy black knickers in their entirety, and one of those bras with holes around the nipple area. I envisaged watching Paul getting it on with this woman, who I worked out was a prostitute. I already caught the footnotes on Paul and my sister. How much worse could it be to watch Paul with a prostitute?

Instead of the act of straightforward sex I expected to witness, he pulled his shirt over his head, not even bothering to undo the bottom buttons. The woman picked up a whip and struck him across the chest. He grunted, in a mixture of pain and pleasure. At first, I wanted to whip him too, but my desire was inspired by anger. I also wanted to turn away, but I knew I needed to witness how the scene would to play out. Paul was into something kinky and I needed all the details, so that I could move on with my life, or in this case my death.

Half an hour later, I had learnt he liked to be whipped before tying up women and insult them while pleasuring himself — which led to him showering the prostitute when he reached a climax. Then he released her from the chains, paid her, offering extra for the soiled underwear she wore. That was my answer. I hadn't been engaged to a murderer. I was engaged to a pathetic excuse for a man with weird fetishes, that if he had tried out on me, I would have chained him up and left him there.

It was light when I stepped outside. I remembered my mum moving home. Worried that I might never find her again if I didn't know where she was, I thought of her and the house where I grew up.

I appeared there. My head spun as if I had a hangover. My mum was still there; watching and yelling instructions to the removal men while they carried her boxes and furniture. I looked around the almost empty house, noticing they had almost finished packing everything into the two large vans parked outside. The carpets remained in the living room and bedrooms, but every piece of furniture was gone. I wanted to cry as I looked around.

I saw brief flashes of me and Emma playing board games in our shared bedroom. They were like stray memories of the past. She laughed at something I said, then the image was replaced by us fighting over clothes she borrowed but never returned. My sister had been worth more than a few fashionable tops or dresses though, hadn't she? We should have been close, I was older by three years. I should have looked out for her. I didn't entirely blame myself for her sneaking around behind my back with Paul. Although, I knew I must have been distant enough as a sister, to make her think it was something she could do without guilt. If we had been close like proper sisters, she never could have considered doing that to me.

I turned and left the bedroom, later stepping into the van with furniture to see where it would take me.

The journey wasn't too long. When the van stopped and the removal men opened the back doors, I recognised the house we were parked outside. It was where my mum's friend Martin lived at the other side of Stretford. Why would she be moving in with him?

I stepped out of the van as my mum parked up in her white mini, then Martin stepped out of the semi-detached house. She threw her arms around him, planting a kiss on his lips.

"What?" I questioned.

Mum never dated after Dad died. I admit we drifted apart, but why didn't she tell me about this? Things must be serious for her to move in with him.

Does Emma know? The question popped into my head. Of course she couldn't. I may not have known much about my sister, but I'm sure she would have said something to me. The last time we'd spoke more than a few lines of meaningful conversation to each other, it was about Dad's death. She never asked to see him before he died; maybe because he was too young, but Emma kept asking me if I visited him in hospital. Mum wouldn't answer her questions about Dad's final days, and I couldn't. She complained so much to me about Mum. It may be the only thing Emma and I ever agreed on.

Something like Mum moving on with someone else would warrant a disgruntled conversation from Emma.

I wanted to know who knew about this, and how and when it happened, but a rush of dizziness sprung on me — as if I might be about to faint.

"Ghosts can't faint," I told myself.

I decided I should get back to Steve. He would know what to do. That was my last thought before I fell endlessly. I questioned if I could be plummeting into an abyss.

Steve stood there, staring at me when the dizziness subsided some time later.

"Where have you been?"

"I went to find out the truth about Paul, then to watch my mum move, because I didn't want to lose track of her."

"You've been gone nearly three weeks," he told me.

I explained everything in detail; from finding out about Paul's twisted desires to my mum having a secret relationship with Martin and her moving in with him, then the extreme dizziness and what like felt a descent into hell.

"I might have some idea what could have happened," he said, reaching for a book.

"Well you won't find answers about my mum and Paul in there," I stated.

"I meant about the missing time. Paul's obviously a creep and your mum didn't feel like she could tell you about Martin, because of the way you reacted when your dad was dying. I don't need a book to tell you that."

I wanted to argue, but he was right about Paul, and my mum too. As much as I hated to admit it, I saw the past play out in front of me at Mum's old house. I gave her so much hassle when she was most likely trying to protect me.

"Why haven't I seen any other ghosts?" I asked, remembering my earlier question.

"Ghosts rarely see each other," he responded.

"There could be one in this room and…" I began. "Is there? Apart from me, I mean."

"No, I avoid them as much as possible."

'Would you tell me if the ghost of my dad ever showed up?"

"If I knew he was your dad." He nodded his head, then quoted from the book in his hands. 'If a ghost expends too much energy in a short period of time, he or she will need to recuperate. No living person can say for sure where a ghost disappears to when this occurs."

"You mean all the travelling from place to place drained me?" I asked.

"Something like that. What did you see when you were falling?"

"I don't know. I felt faint. Then I was falling, then I was here."

Rather than focus on this, I turned my attention back to my murder investigation. Paul hadn't killed anyone. That meant somebody else had and I still didn't know who.

"Did the police find who killed the woman last...I mean, three weeks ago."

"No."

He told me there hadn't been another murder yet, but the police had visited my sister to ask her more questions about me and the woman who was murdered three weeks earlier.

"How do you know that?" I questioned.

"You disappeared," he told me. "I continued investigating your murder. Emma placed an ad for someone to ghost-write a book for her. I got in touch and told her I studied journalism. I may have forgotten to mention dropping out before graduating. I needed paid work anyway."

His answer surprised me. Steve was a recluse and I couldn't blame him, when ghosts popped up everywhere, just like that mole game in the amusement arcades. I knew it must have taken a lot for him to put himself out there. I was also aware how nosy Emma was and guessed she probably asked Steve a lot of personal questions: questions he couldn't answer truthfully without making himself come across as a nutter. On the other hand though, she liked to talk about herself a lot. If she paid Steve to ghost-write a book for her, she may have been so self-absorbed giving him the info he needed that she didn't get to prod at his personal life.

"She asked what else I worked on. I told her the truth, mainly ghost writing, and I was contracted not to talk about it," Steve told me.

"We need to stop whoever this guy is from killing again," I told him.

With no more visions and the past three weeks a blur, I had no new information to go on.

"I should go to Emma's. Maybe I can gather a few more details that you couldn't get. People drop their guard when they're not being watched," I suggested.

"Maybe, but…" Steve looked down at the ground.

He was clearly reluctant to tell me something.

"Whatever it is, I need to know if it's about my murderer."

"Not exactly, but Emma moved in with Paul."

That changed everything. I had two things on my to do list.

"Great, now I need to solve my own murder before the killer adds another victim to his list, and I need to make Emma see what a creep Paul is and move back out. He might not be a killer, but he's not the man I…she thinks he is."

"Good luck with that. Relationships aren't really my area of expertise," Steve pointed out.

I was about to transport myself to Paul's, to spy on Emma, when I remembered the three weeks I lost due to overexerting myself,

"I'm going to walk," I said.

'Probably best,' he agreed.

The walk was different to when I was alive. I used to hate walking and would catch the bus everywhere. I paid for a bus pass every month, even though I lived just under four miles from work. I liked knowing I had it if I wanted to go to the shops or out with friends, although I rarely saw them as I got older. We just drifted apart. As I thought about it, it occurred to me I couldn't name anyone I considered to be a friend, or the last good friend I had. It must have been my death messing up my memories. I was sure I had friends at some point, but not recently.

   I walked past a row of shops I must have passed a thousand times on the bus. Everything seemed different on foot, and probably because I was dead. In life, even though I enjoyed chatting with the customers at work, I always avoided eye contact with strangers when I passed them in the street. Now I could stop and watch people as much as I wanted without them even knowing I was there.

   A woman stepped out of the shop with a heavy-looking bag-for-life in each hand. A small orange rolled out of the top, then another. I challenged myself to get them both back into her bag without her ever knowing they had dropped out. I focussed on one. It was so light that it lifted with little effort. I dropped it back into the bag. The second was trickier as she headed towards the bus stop by then, but I managed to float the orange after her before letting it fall into her bag. A little boy looked back with his mouth wide open as his mother tugged at his hand. Nobody else noticed.

Chapter Seven

I knew I should go to Paul's house and try to figure out a way to educate Emma to what he was really like, but I felt a rush of happiness at being helpful for the first time in a long time, even if it was just saving a shopper from losing two oranges. I racked my brains for what else I could do, when a man ran out of the local supermarket. He was a shoplifter. That much was obvious by the bulge in the oversize jacket he wore, despite the bright sun. Oher shoppers wore t-shirts. The security guard pursued him. I spotted a red car, with another man behind the wheel. The shop lifter's attention shifted from the guard to the car as his friend waited behind the wheel to help him make his escape. The guard was too far behind to reach him in time, unless I did something. I had never moved a person before, but thought it was worth a try. I focused on his right leg, trying to pull it down as he ran. I cheered as he tripped when his foot scraped against the bump in the pavement. He laid there winded next to a pile of dog poo, and his face creased in confusion. The red car pulled away. The shop lifter struggled to get to his feet while calling his friend a few choice names. The security guard grabbed the man by one arm and reached under his coat to retrieve a large frozen chicken.

"What were you going to do with that?" the security guard questioned, between excessive breaths.

I couldn't help but snigger. Surely it was obvious that the thief intended to have a slap-up meal for two, with his friend who scarpered at the first sign of trouble. I figured he didn't have plans to perform voodoo on the chicken to bring it back to life and keep it as a pet.

The thief seemed to think the answer was obvious too and didn't provide a response. The guard dragged him inside, aided by a male shopper who decided to lend a hand, now that the situation appeared to be under control. The shopper threw a look back at a blonde woman half his age, who I assumed he wanted to impress.

I carried on walking to Paul's. It was raining when I arrived just in time to see Emma darting inside the house, with both hands lifting her cropped leather jacket over her head. Her usually straight hair had turned into a frizzy mess. I smiled, my own hair unaffected by the rain and actually looking neater than it had when I was alive.

Paul's car wasn't parked in the driveway, meaning he must be at work. I followed Emma inside, then looked for anything to suggest that Paul had convinced my younger sister to get involved with his fetishes. There was no sign of whips, chains, kinky underwear or anything else unusual as I wandered into each room and looked around.

It was getting late in the afternoon. Paul could be back from work at any time.

The sound of cascading water came from the bathroom across the hallway. Emma was in the shower, I guessed. An idea popped into my head, from a couple of horror movies Paul used to make me watch.

I remembered one night, sat on the sofa together. I felt happy just to sit there and brush my arm against his, whenever I reached over for popcorn. There was the excuse to bury my face into his shoulder whenever a scary scene happened in the film.

"That would never work in real life," Paul's voice rang in my head, reminding me how he really had no idea about anything. I questioned why I had been so needy. Even not knowing what I learnt after my death, we didn't have anything in common. How did I not see that when I was alive?

I entered the bathroom, hearing Emma singing an upbeat pop song as she stood in the shower. I hoped this worked. It would be satisfying for me to prove Paul wrong, even if there was no way of him knowing I proved him wrong.

I was grateful the shower curtain was pulled along. I had no desire to see my sister naked in the shower. I looked at the bathroom mirror as it steamed up. I could use Paul's tooth brush on the sink to write if I could lift it and gain enough control. What should I write?

"Paul is a pervert" seemed like a good option, but she would want to know why.

Everything I wanted to say wouldn't fit on the small space of the mirror on the bathroom cabinet. Instead, I decided to write the address Paul had gone to the night I followed him. Emma was curious about things. She would want to find out why an address she didn't recognise was on the bathroom mirror. Hopefully, she would assume Paul wrote it on the mirror and hadn't thought to wipe it off.

I had to up my concentration levels as I controlled the tooth brush. Stupidly, I grabbed for the sink as I felt dizzy, but my hand slid straight through it. I sensed I was about to pass out, which for me meant blinking out of existence again. I forced my drooping eyes to open and used every bit of mental strength I could gather, to finish writing the address. The last sound I heard before feeling myself fading were Emma stepping out of the shower, her feet sloshing against the floor, then a sharp intake of breath. She must have seen the mirror, I thought to myself, while wondering how long I would be gone for this time.

I reappeared in a basement, a little dazed, but I understood from the previous time, I was just coming back from wherever I went when I experienced a blackout period. I waited for any recognition of the place I was in. Then it struck me that I was in the basement where I had discovered the truth about Paul. I assumed that was how it worked. I appeared at Steve's house after the first time I blacked out, because that's where I was thinking about. In a similar way, I was so focussed on writing down the address in the mirror that I appeared there.

The whips and chains were stored in a box in the corner. I supposed she must put her toys away when she wasn't playing with them.

Voices drifted from the floor above me. Two females were talking, their volumes increasing as if trying to outdo each other.

I walked up the stairs. At least I couldn't see other ghosts. What if the basement was full of the ghosts of people who had been whipped to death? They might be surrounding me, reliving their sordid deaths and I would never know for sure. It worked both ways though; they couldn't see me either.

When I reached the top, I followed the ever-increasing voices to the hallway near the front door.

It was Emma arguing with Paul's prostitute.

"I can't tell you about my clients," the sex worker yelled. "Why don't you go home and talk to your boyfriend?"

"Because he's not going to admit to this. Please be honest with me, woman to woman, just tell me," my sister pleaded as she waved a photo of Paul, in front of the woman's face. "Was he here or not? Did he buy…did he pay for your…services?"

The woman sighed. "Please leave before I call the police."

"Won't they be interested in your choice of occupation?" Emma snapped.

The woman pushed Emma towards the door. Although, my sister managed to slow down her exit by grabbing at coats hanging in the hallway. They fell to the floor, taking some of the hooks with them.

"Tell her," I snapped, wondering whatever happened to the idea of women sticking together. I assumed she would want to be told if she ever found herself in Emma's position.

The prostitute shuddered and creased up her face as her next words seemed to spill out without her consent.

"He was here, about a dozen times. Sometimes to see me and other times he saw another girl who works from here. She recently turned eighteen and he liked that; someone younger and he paid her twice the amount he paid me for my used lingerie, like hers was any better than mine."

Emma stepped back, speechless for perhaps the first time in her life. I was shocked too, not just by the information that even I hadn't known, but how freely the words came out, as if against her will. I was sure I had done that, although I wasn't sure how.

I wanted to stay and see how things played out, but it occurred to me that whatever I did to make her talk must have taken a lot of power. I had to get back to Steve and start trying to solve my murder before anyone else got killed, and before I blacked out again.

I heard Emma swearing as I thought about Steve's house. I smiled a little, maybe because I managed to warn her, or because I stirred things up in her so-called perfect life. Now she would experience how it felt to be cheated on by Paul.

"Sarah," Steve greeted me.

"Hi, no time to explain, but I've shown Emma what Paul is like. Now let's solve my murder."

He looked at me. His mouth opened, then shut and his eyes narrowed in concern, or perhaps uncertainty.

"What is it?"

"You've been gone five weeks this time. Sarah, two more women ended up…" he stopped talking and walked towards the bigger bookcase. He took out some newspaper clippings from the inside of a black photo album and unfolded them on the coffee table. I knelt to read the words, but the images were self-explanatory. Both women were pictured twice; once smiling and alive and a second time dead with significant injuries. I struggled to believe a newspaper would be allowed to print those images. Wasn't it disrespectful to the families?

"They were killed late at night and out of sight, with similar injuries to yours," Steve said, saving me the trouble of reading. "The families of the victims agreed to those photos. They hoped it might shock members of the public into coming forward, if they knew anything that can catch this sicko."

'Did it work?' I asked, although I would be surprised if he said yes. Steve would have opened with that news if it had.

"No, it only dragged out a bunch of nut jobs who wanted attention, saying they witnessed something, when they were nowhere near the crime scenes at the times these two were killed." He pointed to the images on his coffee table.

"I need to stop this guy," I said.

"About that…" He clammed up again.

"Just tell me," I snapped.

"You're dying," he stated.

"Newsflash, I'm already dead. I'm a ghost, remember?" I forced a laugh, but could see there was more to his words from the serious expression on his face.

"What I mean is, you're a ghost, yes. We both know that," Steve said. "But these powers or whatever you want to call them, touching things and…"

"I wrote in a mirror and made a whore confess Paul's sordid pastimes."

"What?" He shook his head. "Never mind. All of that takes up energy and you don't sleep, so you rest by blinking out of existence for a while. The time you're gone gets longer until you die, as in a ghost death."

"A ghost death?" I asked, certain he was making up the term.

"Okay, so I don't have an official name for it, but this is what I know. You're energy and you can recuperate some spent energy, but not as much as you're using up."

"So, what you're saying is, using energy makes me weaker?" I asked.

"Exactly," he confirmed.

I considered his words for a minute. I hadn't given much thought to what would happen to me as a ghost. I took it for granted that the afterlife was eternal.

Although, after I succeeded in showing Emma what Paul was like, that only left solving my own murder. I told myself it didn't matter after that. It was more than most people could hope to achieve in their lifetime, to stop a killer. If I could do that, maybe my life would have been worth something.

"My life wasn't exactly how I thought it was," I told Steve. "If my afterlife is on a timer, then I want to stop this freak and make all of this mean something. You don't have to help me though." I realised I would use up energy quicker without him, but I didn't feel right dragging him into my mess. I had begun to think of him as a friend.

He looked at me, then shrugged. "What the hell? I'm in. My life is exactly what I think it is; lousy. Let's make both of our existences mean something."

I almost felt like there should be an inspirational theme tune playing at that moment, or a montage of us taking down the bad guys together — even though that's not how things worked out.

I grinned at him. "I'd high-five you, but I've got to conserve energy," I stated.

He nodded. "So where do we start?"

"The scene of the last crime," I told him.

"I'm still in, but why? The police will have taken any evidence by now."

"I know. You said I'm connected to the killer because he killed me too. So, let's test out that theory," I suggested, heading toward the door.

I only looked back to confirm Steve was following me. He grabbed his coat from the stand near the door.

Chapter Eight

"What are we doing here?" Steve asked.

I had convinced him to take me to the place where the police found the body of the most recent victim.

"You said I'm connected to the killer. I thought I might get another vision here."

He looked at me without saying anything. I thought he was about concocting a sarcastic response about how stupid my idea was, or about to point out that's not how it works. I tried to come up with a counter-argument as I racked my brain for another idea, because I didn't know any other method to suggest for finding the killer.

"That's possible actually," he said when he finally spoke.

"Really?"

"Yes." He nodded. I made out his head movement because of the light from the torch he held. "Just look around and see if anything triggers a vision."

I walked further down the alley, with Steve walking behind me providing the light. There was a large bin to my left and another further along to my right. Nothing unusual about that. I stood in the space between two buildings. One was a nightclub, the other was a popular takeaway restaurant. I asked Steve to point the torch at the floor. I assumed he was right. The police would have found any evidence left behind. It didn't hurt to search it again though.

"This is where he got Valerie," Steve whispered. "They found her body somewhere around here." He pointed to the ground near the side of the restaurant.

"How do you know that?" I questioned.

"The pictures in the paper; they showed her by the wall where she was found. There was graffiti on the wall. This is the only bit of wall on either side with graffiti on."

I looked closer at the graffiti, then at the rest of the building.

"Good spot," I said.

I knelt and examined the area where Valerie's body must have been discovered.

"A cleaner from the club freaked out when she took the rubbish out and found her there. The police report said the body had been there a few hours," Steve told me.

I was impressed by the amount of research he did while I blacked out. I could also imagine how finding a dead body would freak someone out. I wondered who found me.

"Did you learn anything about my death?"

"A jogger found your corpse," he said, as if reading my mind. Perhaps that was the obvious thing to wonder. I stifled a laugh.

"What?"

"It's always joggers. Makes you wonder whether everyone should go to the gym, or play Wii Fit instead of going jogging. Less chance of stumbling across a dead body that way. Better yet, nobody ever finds a dead body on the way to the cake shop," I pointed out.

I focussed my attention on the ground. As I suspected, there was nothing to suggest someone was killed there; no traces of blood or signs of a struggle. I began to think my idea wasn't so good after all. How was I meant to pluck a vision out of the air as if by magic? I was about to stand and ask Steve if he wanted to go home, before an idea inserted itself into my mind.

I concentrated on making my hand connect with the ground as I lowered my arm. My hand passed through the concrete several times before I felt the damp surface against my fingers and palm. I laughed. That would have grossed me out when I was alive, touching the ground in a dodgy alley where drunk people had urinated, spit or excreted other bodily fluids. In death I was grateful to touch anything, even something so unhygienic.

"Maybe you shouldn't use your energy like..." Steve began.

I didn't hear the rest of what he said because I saw myself in the sane alley, but without Steve. I thought I was about to relive my own murder.

A gust of wind sent hair flying across my face. Black hair, like Valerie's, not red like mine. I guessed I was reliving her final moments then. It wasn't the way I expected any vision to go. Dying hadn't gone the way I expected either. Why would this be any different? Footsteps pounded against the ground, getting louder as they grew closer. Panic rose up in the pit of my stomach, escalating until my head spun, or at least it seemed that way, then I noticed the knife and lifted my hands in defence as he aimed the weapon at my throat. I felt my belly tear being torn open as he redirected the blade there. Warm liquid, I figured it must be blood, leaked from the wound. My hands went to it without any command from me. I pulled them away, grabbing at the man as if trying to mark him with his crime. He grabbed my arms and pinned them to my side. I screamed out, trying to kick my attacker — missing as he moved backwards. The pain in my stomach intensified when I dragged the knife out, hoping to use it as a weapon against him. More blood drizzled out of the open wound. I pressed one hand against the gash as if I could not only stop the blood but also make it return to my body where it belonged. I waved the knife at him with my other hand. He laughed a familiar laugh, but nothing like Paul's

He ran at me. It happened so fast. Somehow, he wrestled the knife out of my hand without me succeeding in drawing even a drop of blood from him. Then he stabbed me again, further up this time. I spluttered, realising this was it. He had struck something important; I was sure of it. He extracted the knife again, then used his right arm to push me onto the ground. The force behind it was more than necessary. I was already light-headed from the rapid blood loss resulting from the second cut.

I lay there, unable to move — feeling physically burdened by the knowledge that would be the last place I ever saw. I always wanted to go to Disneyland someday, but that would never happen now. My attacker stood over me.

He knelt and whispered, "women like you shouldn't be allowed to live. Just know, you brought this on yourself."

His face leaned in close to mine as he kissed my cheek. The smell of chocolate orange brownies laced with cinnamon were on his breath. As the vision faded, I understood why I recognised the scent. When I worked at The Crusty Edge with Paul, he asked me to come up with some new dessert options. Out of the recipes I tried to bake, he preferred my chocolate orange brownies with a hint of cinnamon. As far as I knew, nobody else nearby sold them, not using my recipe anyway. The smell was distinguishable. If we had the brownies on show behind the glass counter, the smell wafted through the restaurant and the sight of them resulted in triple the usual number of dessert orders.

"Sarah, Sarah," Steve's voice snapped me back to the present moment.

I looked at him, feeling dazed and confused. It was almost as if I had been Valerie, with my own memories pushed to the back of my mind — before my memories of the brownie scent had brought them all back as Valerie faded, but still lingered there in the back of my mind. Steve's voice made Valerie disappear completely, until I became only myself again.

"What happened? You were screaming and kicking out, then you stopped moving and your eyes stared at me, only it was more like you were staring through me. I thought you were dead, like a corpse I mean," Steve explained.

"I saw Valerie's last moments. It worked," I announced. I quickly told him everything, fearing I might forget or worse, disappear long enough for more women to be murdered. I felt dizzy, so Steve insisted we stayed for a few hours. The look on his face as he watched me almost constantly, told me he also thought I might disappear in front of his eyes.

"That was stupid," he said. "Something like that takes an enormous amount of energy."

"I know, I know," I replied. I understood I was using up energy, but didn't know how much was used on each thing I did. Neither did Steve. He knew it was a lot though. "Can we go now?" I asked, eager to get back to his house and put the pieces together.

"Fine, but don't start complaining to me if you blink out of existence permanently."

"You do know I wouldn't be able to complain to you if....never mind." I shook my head, knowing he didn't like to have long conversations with me in public. I doubted anyone would find it so strange at that time of night. Anyone out so late would assume he was drunk, then cross the road to avoid him.

We arrived back at the house. Steve left me alone for a few minutes while he went down to the basement, returning with a huge whiteboard.

"I thought we would put all the clues on here, like in the movies," he suggested.

"Okay," I agreed, secretly impressed. It almost felt like having a guest role in an episode of one of my favourite crime shows, if the protagonists solving the crime were a recluse who saw dead people and one of those same dead people. Maybe it wasn't too similar to my much-loved crime shows after all.

Steve took an A4 sketchpad from the top of one of his bookcases, picked up some coloured pencils and began to draw. I looked over his shoulder while he leaned on the coffee table, kneeling on the floor. He sketched the alley, then he looked up at me and asked me to confirm where I had stood during the vision when I relived Valerie's murder.

I told him where I started after the guy cornered me, and where I ended up after he stabbed me twice, then shoved me as I bled out — all relived through my vision as though I experienced myself, rather than just watching Valerie's last moments.

Steve drew a sequence of images, then used Blu-Tack to attach them to the whiteboard. The pictures seemed as realistic as drawings could be, serving as a reminder of the events I experienced in my vision. I would struggle to ever forget them though. It felt like looking at the illustrations for a graphic novel I previously lived out. It would need to be 18+ rated though.

"And the smell?" Steve asked, even though I already told him.

"I definitely smelt my brownies, well not mine anymore. I didn't bake the one he ate, because I've been busy being dead, but they're my recipe."

"You might know this guy if he ate at your restaurant."

"I probably chatted to him. The customers liked a chat, or at least I thought they did," I said — remembering the words Martha used, when she requested anyone but me to take her order. "Maybe I annoyed him by chatting too much, when he just wanted to eat his brownies in peace," I suggested.

"That wouldn't explain why he killed the others," Steve reason.

I was a little put out that he didn't attempt to argue that I wasn't annoying, or even say he liked me talking. Maybe I did talk too much, I admitted to myself.

Steve had a point though, it didn't explain the other victims, but we knew he ate at my former workplace before killing Valerie. It was a good assumption to say he ate at The Crusty Edge at least once while I was still alive.

"That will be where he first noticed me," I suggested. It made sense. It was the only place I went regularly. I didn't have a favourite place to go with friends, or even alone. Paul had been enough for me, or at least that's what I believed back then. The reason the killer seemed familiar had to be because he was a customer.

"Did you see his face in the vision?" Steve asked.

"No, it was dark. And he had a hat on, so I can't even tell you the colour of his hair, if he had any."

"What kind of hat?" Steve asked.

I ended up describing the man's attire to Steve as he sketched an image of the killer. A dark coloured beanie hat. Jacket, in khaki or dark denim and jeans, although I wasn't sure of that one. As I didn't have much of a description to give Steve, he came up with a surprisingly good resemblance of him. The colours of his clothing didn't seem right, but it was as close as he could get with so little information to go on.

"Why don't you do this for a living," I asked him.

"Right, working for the police, drawing suspects in criminal cases including murder; because what could go wrong in that job for someone with my sight?"

I understood what he meant. If he had to work on a murder case, and the victim's ghost hadn't moved on; Steve would be the obvious target for the ghost to latch onto. It was likely he would be the only one around with the ability to see the victim.

"Sorry," I said.

"You can't understand what it's like and how much it gets in the way of any kind of normal life, unless you suffer from this so-called gift of mine. No offense to you. You're not too much of a pest. And this mission of yours to find the killer has actually given me something to get out of bed for in the morning."

I looked at him, waiting for that sarcastic smile, but it never materialised.

"That was almost a compliment," I said.

"Don't get me wrong. I'll be glad when it's over and I can drink myself back into a drunken stupor," he replied, but the sadness in his eyes suggested he didn't completely mean it.

Chapter Nine

I convinced Steve to visit The Crusty Edge, under the guise of being a freelance journalist, looking for interviews with Graham (the manager), the other staff and a selection of customers. I knew Paul would go for that; to get his name in the paper and have his colleagues and customers singing his praises. He wasn't usually boastful when we were together, but if we ever got onto the subject of cooking, Paul would compare himself favourably against the likes of Gordon Ramsey and Jamie Oliver.

I hoped Steve might stumble across the murderer, or at least someone who saw him eating there.

"I don't know what questions I'm meant to ask that can help me uncover who this guy is. How about; did you happen to notice anyone drawing a plan of action to murder someone while you were having a romantic meal?" Steve asked.

"I dare you to ask someone that question," I retorted, accustomed to his sarcasm by that point.

"Just don't talk to me when we get there," he told me.

His request didn't offend me. I understood by then, what it was like for him to be seen talking to someone in public when nobody else could see that person.

***

I was on my best behaviour and remained silent as Steve started his interviews.

Paul volunteered to go first. I watched him as he sat at the small table in the cramped staff canteen.

His eyes were blood-shot as if he had been crying or gone without sleep for a long time. I guessed Emma had left him. She must have, I thought. I couldn't speak to Steve to get him to ask that, even if there was a way of him sneaking that question into the interview.

"How long have you worked here?" Steve asked the first question, opening his notepad in preparation for writing down the response.

"I started eight years ago as a waiter, but the chef fell ill a few weeks later and I offered to step in. They recognised how good I am and took me on as a chef on a part time basis, while I worked as a waiter the rest of the time. The chef left not long after. He obviously didn't like the competition and the job became mine full-time." Paul laughed in fake modesty, but I remembered how much he liked to brag over his cooking skills.

I also recalled a different version of his story, involving him pleading with Graham to give him a chance when the chef fell ill. After the chef returned to work, everything seemed to go wrong for the poor guy. Looking back, it seemed too much of a coincidence to think Paul had nothing to do with that.

Steve scribbled a few notes in his pad, then asked, "your family must have been proud of that?"

"My parents died when I was young, but my fiancée…" he stopped talking, swallowed hard, then spoke again. "A few people close to me were proud."

"Would you say this is a community restaurant? Do you have returning customers?"

"We're in the heart of the city, but we still get a lot of familiar faces and some new ones too. I'm behind the scene a lot, so I couldn't tell you their names. The waiting staff know some of the regulars on a first name basis though. It makes them feel special, so yes, in some ways I suppose it is a community restaurant."

The next few interviews were with new members of staff, some so new that I didn't recognise them from when I was alive and working there. One of the newbies mentioned a man when Steve asked him about regular customers.

"He creeps some of the waitresses and female kitchen staff out," James, the waiter said.

"How does he do that?" Steve questioned, in a flat tone, trying to make the question sound like he was making small talk, rather than planning to use anything about the creepy customer in his article.

This seemed to relax James. He sat back in his chair and said, "he's been here a few times during my shift, but he never talks to me. It's always the female staff he sidles up to. Two have left because of him. They complained to Paul and Graham, but neither seemed to care. It's all about profits here. Graham even said a small amount of attention is to be expected and encouraged because it brings in the tips, which he so graciously allows us to divide amongst ourselves at the end of the night."

"That doesn't sound so bad, if the customers are just chatting up the staff, but not causing any harm, right?" Steve pressed.

"That's the thing. Shelly, the counter assistant, is sure he tried to follow her home one night. He hung around long after he finished his meal and last drink of wine. He didn't make any move to leave until it was almost time for Shelly to clock off. He was extra chatty with her all night, but she just remained friendly, though not too familiar. She didn't want to lead him on."

"Go on," Steve said, when James paused.

"Shelly called me and said she heard someone following her. I stayed on the phone while I got into the car. I only live a five-minute drive away from where she was. I went to pick her up. I had to slow down while I looked out for her. That's when I saw someone run down an alley. It was dark, but it might have been him."

"Do you know his name?" Steve asked.

"This isn't anything to do with the article you're writing, is it?" The man suddenly seemed uncertain. I guess he felt concerned about the possibility of losing his job.

"No, but a freelance journalist friend of mine might find this useful for his article. When you're working as a freelance, you have to look out for each other. I wouldn't mention your name to him though," Steve promised.

"Good. I overheard him tell some of the girls his name is Christopher, but to others he calls himself Johnny. Something needs to be done about him. Shelly was terrified after that. She changed all her shifts to match mine."

***

"What are you thinking?" Steve asked when we were back at his house and we could talk freely again.

"What if that's what he does, frequents different places and finds his victims that way?"

"But how does he pick them?"

"Maybe he doesn't like rejection," I suggested.

"James never said Shelly rejected the guy," Steve said.

"When women have to work with people like that and they try to be friendly, while keeping them at a distance, it's a rejection as far as some guys are concerned," I insisted.

"So, he picks his victims based on those who reject him?" Steve asked.

"I'm not saying he does for sure, but it's a possibility," I said. "And he didn't get to Shelley, because James got there in time and scared him away."

I did my best to convince Steve that Christopher, Johnny, or whatever his real name really was, might try to get to Shelly again. We knew her shift matched James's shift. He wouldn't be able to follow her after work. He might try again sometime when she wasn't going to or from work. James couldn't be with her all the time. The other option was, the killer might decide it wasn't worth the hassle and move onto another victim, which we would miss if we got too caught up in trying to protect Shelly.

"Assuming this guy is the killer, and not just some random weirdo, like Paul for example."

I glared at Steve for dropping that reminder into the conversation. I thought I was moving on from Paul and his previously hidden obsessions with whips, bondage and used lingerie. Splitting up the relationship between him and my sister had brought some satisfaction, though probably not the same amount he received at that brothel he frequented.

Emma had been left reeling from all the lies and the sneaking around though. I hadn't completely forgiven her, but I knew I should have been the kind of sister she wouldn't have wanted to steal a man from. By showing the real Paul, it was my late attempt at being a better sister. Better from beyond the grave than never, maybe.

"Yeah, thanks for that reminder," I told Steve.

He looked unsure of himself — possibly realising he touched a nerve with his last comment. "Why don't you haunt the restaurant for a while to see if he comes back? I'll try to find out if he's a regular anywhere else."

"How are you going to do that?"

He switched on the computer and searched for restaurants and bars in the City Centre. "All the murders so far took place within a two-mile radius of the restaurant where you used to work. This guy could be getting his victims from other places too. So, I'll compile a list and speak to the staff for a freelance article on creepy customers. I'll say it's about raising awareness of harassment in the workplace."

"Really? That's a lot of work and…" I began.

"I know, but I'll write the article, for real and send it to a few publications. I need the money anyway."

"You do that, even though you didn't graduate?" I asked.

"I can't work a nine-to-five because of my unique condition. I need to make money somehow though," he stated.

I should have known he worked as a freelance journalist and wasn't just posing as one to get information. It was another confirmation of how self-absorbed I could be. I felt pleased that his education, despite being cut short, still benefitted him. I never pursued a career in Journalism, despite finishing with a 2.1.

"When this is over, we should go for a drink," I suggested. "I mean. You'll drink, and I'll sit and listen to you tell me about yourself, and it'll be here in your house, so you don't look like a crazy person talking to yourself."

"Are you hitting on me?" he asked.

"No, I'm just trying to stop being so self-absorbed."

"And how's that working out?" he asked, with a small smile which made his green eyes sparkle a little.

"It's a work in progress," I replied.

I went back to the restaurant to watch and wait for Johnny Christopher, or whoever he was to return.

I recognised James and a few of the newer staff from the interviews Steve had conducted. I spotted Shelly when she entered the staffroom and kissed James before starting her shift. I recalled her starting work a few weeks before I died. She was a waitress back then.

Her hair was red like mine when she started working at the restaurant. She jokingly told me that us redheads need to stick together. A few days later, she became a bottle blonde. I think we would have become friends if I hadn't been murdered, or if I was the kind of person to have female friends. I had a few girls I hung around with at school, but I used to hang around with Paul and his friends. The girls only spoke to me because they fancied one of Paul's friends. I'd introduce them to the boy of their choice. If he liked the girl, I'd tried to set him up with her, then she'd become part of our group. We were never real friends though — not the kind of friends who shared secrets and spent time at each other's houses.

Maybe Shelly would have changed all of that. I was jolted back to an unusually hectic Wednesday night at the restaurant.

Shelly and I were the only waiting staff on duty. The place was packed out to the point where we had to get extra chairs from the storage cupboard to squeeze some of the larger groups around the tables. Other customers were getting frustrated when they had to get past the people on the extra seats — making going to the toilet or popping outside for a smoke more challenging than they preferred it to be. Drinks were spilled over and there was little room or time to clean up in between taking orders and fetching food and more drinks. I asked Graham if he could call in extra staff. He refused. I talked to Paul, but he wouldn't back me up.

"Just do your best, babe. I'm swamped in here too". I did a quick count. There was him and four kitchen staff working on the food orders. He was doing better than me.

His flippancy made me so angry. Shelly must have seen how close I was to either losing my temper at Paul and the manager, or walking out and never coming back.

"It's okay," she told me. Her calm voice almost soothed me as we stood side by side, facing all the customers. Half of them still waiting for us to take their food and drink orders. "You take the hundred on the left. I'll take the hundred on the right."

I couldn't help smiling. The number of hungry diners wasn't quite that high. My eyes went to the nearest table. A man sat alone, leaving three unoccupied seats around his table. At the rate he was eating his chocolate orange and cinnamon brownie, he might be finished by Christmas…next year.

"Sir, would you mind moving to one of the stools if it's only you. We're unusually busy tonight and people might need the table." I pointed towards the unoccupied tables, which were at the far-left side of the restaurant. They were higher than the normal tables, with red stools in front of them.

"But I get a better view from here," he said. His eyes seemed to drill right through me. Why hadn't I picked up on the way he appeared to be mentally undressing me when this happened? Watching it all play out, with every word and action out of my control, seemed to help me focus on the details I hadn't picked up on the first time.

This was him, my killer. I just knew it.

Chapter Ten

"You could join me at this table, then I wouldn't be alone," he suggested. The way his lips twisted into a sinister smile, made me shudder.

"Oh, I can't," I feigned disappointment. "I'm working and we're so busy, plus I'm engaged to the head chef. We don't want him to spit in your food or anything, do we?" I smiled in the way I had often practised in front of the mirror. A smile reserved for awkward customers or situations where I had to be polite, while secretly wanting to tell someone where to go.

"They all say that, they always have a boyfriend or a husband," he said, smiling again, but it was another cold smile which didn't reach his eyes. They were full of aggression and made me uncomfortable.

"Sorry," I said, moving onto the next table while he muttered something incoherent.

By the time I returned to check on him and have another attempt at convincing him to move tables, he had gone.

My trip down memory lane skipped forward a few hours to the end of my shift. Paul's lack of support angered me, when I'd suggested to Graham that we might need extra staff. Instead of having a drink and waiting until Paul's shift finished an hour after mine, I walked home, hoping the exercise would help me vent some of my frustration. I hated being angry at him.

I hadn't gone far before I heard heavy footsteps striking the pavement behind me. Thinking it might be Paul, I turned around. I should have known better. He would never leave work early, even if I was mad at him. We would talk about things at home later, then he usually promised to do things differently next time, if he had done something to upset me.

"Hey," the man from the restaurant said.

"Run," I thought, but of course I didn't, because that's not what I did the first time this happened. I stood there, like a deer caught in the head lights.

"I knew you didn't have a fiancé. If you did, he'd be walking you home now."

I saw the glint of a knife, like in the visions I had of the other victims. This time I was about to become the victim.

I stumbled back, almost tripping on a loose paving stone, but I kept backing up. For each back-step I took, he stepped forward two or three steps. I turned and ran, although too late. I didn't get more than a few strides before his hand clutched at my arm and dragged me back. I wish I could say I thought of something clever, like the way his hand reminded me of those grabbers at the fair, the ones that always drop the prize right before opening over the hatch. I didn't think that though. My thoughts were a jumbled mess. The experience was terrifying and unnerving. He pulled me towards him and I was aware of how this would end, armed with my knowledge and already being dead, but I was trapped in the moment of what was happening, unable to do anything that might change the course of events. I felt his body pressing against mine and the excited breathing against the back of my neck.

"You should have given me a chance. You girls are all the same."

"Please," I pleaded.

"I'm doing the male population a favour by getting rid of the cock teases," he said, holding the knife to my throat.

My body stiffened as he clamped his hands around my arms. Then I struggled, which only seemed to amuse him.

"What are…" I began to ask, but he covered my mouth with his. I should have bitten his tongue when he fished the chewing gum from my mouth. The sick freak pocketed it like a keepsake.

I screamed. His hand smothered the noise. I bit down then. He gasped, although I couldn't tell whether it was from the pain or a perverse pleasure.

I experienced every cut, hit and touch as he alternated between groping, slashing and hitting out at me. I tried to fight back, but he was too strong and each impact from his fist or cut from his knife left me weaker. By the time it was over, all I was able to do was lie on the ground watching him as his gloved hands touched me through my clothes, in places only Paul had ever touched. Without warning, I lost control of my senses and went numb. Perhaps I was already so close to death that my body went into shock, or maybe I just accepted the inevitability of it all.

I scrunched my eyelids shut, finding myself at Steve's house when I opened them again. His eyes widened when he saw me. Concern spread across his face as he approached me.

"No joke intended, but you look like you've seen a ghost," he said.

"I saw my own death replayed, almost as if I was actually there, but without the power to change anything. Does that count as seeing a ghost?" I asked.

"Shit," he responded, looking shocked and curious at the same time. "I've never read about anything like that happening."

"I'd love to stay and tell you all about it. You could write a book of your own, to add to all of these," I suggested, pointing to his full bookshelves. "I have to get back to the restaurant though. Shelly could be in danger."

He looked me up and down, then said, "I should go. You might need to recover some lost energy."

"I'm fine," I told him, although I felt the familiar dizziness threatening to take over.

"You're not fine, you're transparent," he argued.

"Oh please, like you really know me or…"

"No, I mean you're literally transparent, like the typical ghost cliché," he insisted.

"What?"

"You looked like any other person before, corporeal until you tried to pick anything up at least, but now you're see-through like you're fading away."

"Oh," is all I replied. I wasn't sure what it meant, or how I was supposed to react to the news of my transparency.

"You stay here. I'll go to The Crusty Edge," he replied.

I didn't argue. Instead, I watched helplessly as he grabbed his coat and left. I felt grateful to him for helping me, of course I was. I just hated the feeling of being unable to do anything for myself. I wondered what I was supposed to do while Steve was busy protecting Shelly. She was my almost friend.

The dizziness threatened to take over again. I let myself slump to the ground, falling through the floor, then I continued to plummet. Needless to say, it didn't help with the dizziness at all. I blacked out again. When I came to, I was in a house I didn't recognise. The furniture looked in good condition, but dated, like an older person's furniture.

"Can you check the attic to see if my cups are up there?" I heard a familiar voice ask.

Mum? I wondered.

Martin walked past the doorway of the living room where I stood, then his footsteps headed up the stairs as the bannister creaked, presumably under his weight. He never was a sporty person. I used to go running, even though I hated it. I believed it was important to keep in shape though. I thought it would stop Paul's eyes from wandering if I tried to eat healthier and do regular exercise. How wrong was I? It turned out Paul sought his regular exercise somewhere else. So anyway, back to Martin. He was always hanging around my mum, but I never thought she would consider him as more than a friend. My dad was the complete opposite to Martin. Dad had been athletic and played football with a local pub team every week. He looked good for his age. Some girls at my school fancied him, which grossed me out and is probably another reason I didn't want to make friends with other girls. I didn't want them to be my friends for the sole reason of going to my house to gawp at my dad. So, I pushed people away.

Martin was nothing like Dad. I couldn't figure out why Mum shacked up with him, but assumed it had to be part of a plan to avoid getting hurt. As far as I was concerned, there was no way she could love Martin. If something happened to him, it wouldn't hurt as much; the way it did when Dad died.

"They weren't there," I heard Martin tell my mum, jolting me out of my thoughts.

"Well, I…" the doorbell cut her off mid-sentence.

"Are you expecting another parcel?" Martin asked my mum.

"No," she replied.

I followed her to the door, curious about what she might have ordered.

"Ms Winters?" a male voice boomed.

"Yes," she replied.

"Can we come in and talk to you about your daughter?"

I looked over my mum's shoulder to see two policemen stood on the doorstep.

"Of course," she said, shuffling out of the way and pulling the door further open.

They stepped inside. She beckoned them towards the living room, where they sat on the two-seat sofa, leaving the chair for my mum. She stood, eying the chair, then the policemen.

"Can I make you a cup of tea?" she asked.

I hoped they wouldn't accept her offer. I wanted to hear what they had to say about me, not just in the usual way that I wanted people to talk about me. I thought maybe they caught the creep who killed me and the others. That meant he wouldn't kill again, and I would be able to move on to whatever came next for me.

"No thanks," they both said, almost in unison.

Mum sat, perched on the end of her seat. "You said you had news?"

"Yes, we've arrested a person of interest, following a tip-off."

"What does this mean? Is he the killer? Did he kill my daughter?" my mum fired off a round of questions.

"All we can say is, he was hanging around your daughter's workplace and someone tipped us off," the younger of the policemen stated.

"Yes," I exclaimed, assuming Steve must have tipped them off. He couldn't exactly go to the police station, but he figured out a way to tell the police about Johnny/Christopher. It didn't matter what the freaks real name was. All that mattered was, the police had him. They would find out who he was, then lock him up for a long time, hopefully forever.

"Who? It doesn't mean he killed anyone though, surely. Lots of people eat there," my mum pointed out.

"Of course," the older man agreed. "However, when we followed up the lead and spoke to your other daughter, she told us that she hired him to ghost write a book for her and he kept asking questions about Sarah, even though that wasn't the subject matter for her book."

I stared at the two of them. Emma hired Steve to write her book. They couldn't be talking about him though.

"Are you sure?" I was pleased with my mum for not sounding convinced.

"It's not him, Mum. Tell them they've got the wrong man, please."

"Why would he do that? If he killed my daughter and those other women, why would he draw attention to himself by hanging around the restaurant and my younger daughter?"

In that moment, I wanted to hug my mum for asking the sensible question.

"Sometimes killers return to the scene of the crime," the older man said. "He may feel intense guilt, or perverse pleasure by hiding in plain sight. I'm not a psychologist. It's also possible he's not the guy who killed the other women, but it is suspicious."

"But…I…" she started, then forced her mouth shut.

"We just wanted to give you an update. We'll question him and call you if anything materialises out of his arrest."

"Like his innocence," I shouted after them, as they said goodbye to my mum, then left her distraught on the doorstep.

Chapter Eleven

I followed my mum as she walked to the bus stop. I couldn't help wondering why she never learned how to drive, but it wasn't the most pressing issue at that moment. Hopefully, she was going to the police station. Although, I wouldn't have been surprised if she popped in to gossip to one of her friends and tell them all about how all this had upset her so much. I considered her to be an ice queen after she never acted upset over Dad's death, unless I asked why. Then she would become upset, but it was all an act, wasn't it?

To my amazement, she went to Urmston police station. The way she pushed open both doors and let them slam shut after her, then marched up to the desk, I thought she might end up having a fist fight with the lady behind the front desk.

"Can I help you?" The woman asked, her voice raised a little and her hands rested on her hips as if trying to show authority.

My mum either didn't notice or chose to ignore the way the desk lady, and the two-men sat down waiting to be seen, were looking at her. The place was in complete silence.

"The suspect in my daughter's murder, I want to see him," Mum barked.

The woman's eye's opened wider. I wasn't sure who felt more surprised; her or me. The two men whispered among themselves and one eyed my mum in a way that would have made me feel uncomfortable if anyone looked at me that way.

"Can I ask for your daughter's name, madam?"

"Surely you should know. Do you have a lot of…" my mum started to ask, but stopped, probably remembering there had been a number of murdered women in the local news. She would have to narrow it down. "Sarah Winters."

"Okay. Well, I'm sorry for your loss of course, but we can't let you see the suspect. It could interfere with any future court case."

"Can you at least tell me his name?"

"Sorry, but we can't…"

"Well, what use are you?" Mum demanded.

I had to admit to myself, I was impressed. I had never seen her so worked up before. If it was an act, she had me fooled.

"They've got the wrong man, Mum. Tell them they've got the wrong person," I said.

"What if you've got the wrong one and the real one is running around out there still killing women? That blood will be on your hands," she threatened.

"Please, calm down. We know how to do our jobs and if the suspect is innocent, we will find out."

"That is not reassuring," my mum muttered, "not at all." She stormed out of the police station in the same dramatic fashion as she had entered.

I started to go after her, but stopped before reaching the door. I wanted to know what she would do next, but the woman behind the desk couldn't see me. Just to make sure, I waved at her while she scowled and muttered something about the door being almost banged off its hinges, as if the door and its precious hinges held more importance than my murder case, or any other murder case for that matter. I knew I could get to see Steve while my mum couldn't. I walked past the desk and through walls and doors until I found the cells. He was still there, sat alone in a cell. The cell opposite was occupied by a man who looked about sixty, but might be younger. He sat slumped against the wall, laughing to himself, possibly drunk or high. Either way, he wasn't fit to judge if Steve started talking to a ghost.

"Steve," I whispered from outside his cell, in an attempt not to startle him. He sat on his poor excuse for a bed. "Don't say anything, just hold up your fingers to answer."

The man in the other cell might be too far gone to care, but I remembered there would be cameras.

Steve turned to look at me and nodded.

"How long was I gone?"

He held up two fingers on one hand, then half a finger on the other.

"Two and a half weeks?"

He nodded once.

"How long have you been here?"

He held up a finger, so I guessed he meant a day. They wouldn't hold him at the police station for one week. The police had only just told my mum they had a suspect, so one day made more sense.

"I'm sorry I got you into this, but I'll get you out," I said. I didn't know how I was going to get him out, but I imagined myself using my ghost energy to bend the bars. Then what? If it didn't drain me and send me away again, I would still have to get him past the cops and out of the station. I had no way of fighting them, and I didn't want to. I only wanted to find the real killer.

"Shelly?" I asked.

"Alive, last time I saw her," he whispered.

I understood that didn't mean she was still alive at that moment though.

"Go," he whispered.

I was about to argue, thinking he didn't want anything to do with me anymore. I couldn't blame him. He meant go to Shelly, I realised.

"I'll be back though," I promised.

I returned to the restaurant, taking the shortcut of appearing there, rather than walking. I didn't want to leave Shelly unprotected for any longer than I had to.

I found myself facing the creep. He sat at a table in the middle of the restaurant. I guessed it was early afternoon. The lunchtime buzz was just dying down. A few men in suits and some women in smart/casual dresses were in the stages of leaving; putting on their jackets, heading for the toilets or paying their bills.

My attention shifted back to him – the killer – sitting alone and chatting to Shelly. Her eyes darted towards the leaving customers. I noticed she had changed back to her natural hair colour.

Out of the eighty seats, only four other seats remained occupied. Two young blonde girls sat by the window oblivious to Shelly's dilemma as they laughed together at something on their phones. The kitchen staff would be in the back. A waiter stood in the right corner taking an order from the elderly couple from before. It no longer bothered me that the wife had asked for someone other than me, before discovering there was little chance of me serving her because I was dead. I felt more concerned by the mass murderer chatting up Shelly.

"I have work to do," she said.

He looked around, noticing the almost empty restaurant. James was nowhere to be seen. It wasn't uncommon for the staff to take on extra shifts or for other staff to be off sick. I guessed something like that happened, causing Shelly to be working a different shift to him.

The creep pulled Shelly onto his knee as she struggled to get to her feet.

"It's quiet, you have time," he tried to kiss her.

'I don't even know your name, and I have a boyfriend, James. He's one of the waiters here.'

"I'm Mark," he said. "And I don't see James here now."

That was a new one. I wondered if he introduced himself by a different name to every one of his potential victims. If so, it would be impossible to guide the police to him without finding out his real name.

"Excuse me, sir. Is everything okay?" The waiter walked over.

"I'm fine thanks, I'll just have the bill," Mark said, releasing Shelly as she used the table to pull herself to her feet, almost falling over in her haste to get away.

"Erm, okay," the waiter said. He looked no older than twenty. He seemed to be considering whether to say something else. I assumed he must have seen Mark (as I would stick to calling him for now) molesting Shelly. He shook his head, indicating he thought he had said enough. He walked behind the counter to produce the bill, but kept glancing over at Mark.

Hours later, Shelly's shift ended. I followed her home in case Mark decided to loiter nearby, waiting to do the same. There was no sign of him though. I watched her enter her house, wondering if she and James lived together. A light came on in the bedroom long before Shelly would have time to walk up the stairs. It could be James, I told myself.

Why would he only switch on the light after she shut the front door behind her? There was no valid reason for him to be sitting in the dark waiting until she returned from work.

"Shit," I said, realising it was unlikely to be James waiting in her house so early in their relationship.

I charged at the front door, passed through it and leapt up the stairs two at a time, passing Shelly who was only halfway up the steps by the time I reached the top.

"Stop, turn around and run," I yelled.

She carried on walking because she didn't hear me.

I looked behind me at the light seeping through the gap in the bedroom door. She saw it too and made a tutting sound, probably thinking she had left it on all day.

"No," I yelled. I knew the warning was useless, but what else could I do?

She sped up and pushed the door open, not making it into the bedroom. Mark leapt out at her, pushing her towards the stairs. She would have gone tumbling down them if I hadn't panicked and reached out to grab her. I didn't understand how it happened, but for a few seconds

I was corporeal. I caught her by the arm – preventing her fall.

"What the fuck?" Mark swore. He stared at me.

"Sarah?" Shelly asked. Her eyes widened.

She used the bannister to steady herself, right before I disappeared. I could tell that neither of them were able to see me anymore. Mark glanced around, blinking, then charged at Shelly again. She side stepped into the bathroom and Mark almost continued down the stairs. He grabbed at the bannister. I tried to push him, but my hands passed straight through. I didn't notice Shelly running at him with the bathroom scales until she slammed them against his head. His grip on the bannister loosened. She hit him again, poising herself for a third strike. She missed because he fell back, as if doing an ungraceful backwards somersault down the stairs. The thought occurred to me, if it was rated in The Olympics, the judges would all give the execution of the fall a zero.

"You go, girl," I exclaimed, like I would if I was watching the action unfold on television.

She stood and watch him tumble for a few seconds, before retreating back to the bathroom and locking the door. I could her hear calling the police on her mobile phone. For a moment, I thought this was it. The police were about to arrive and arrest him. They would take prints and DNA to connect him to my murder; then to the other murders. Steve would be freed. I would be free to move on without leaving unfinished business behind. I imagined myself floating up to heaven where I would spend my days watching over everyone, while sitting on a cloud made out of marshmallows.

'Really?' I snapped, seeing movement at the bottom of the stairs. Why did the bad guys always get up again, but the victims seemed to die too easily? I knew I wasn't on television, but the same unfair system seemed to apply in real life too.

Mark used the bottom of the bannister to pull himself up. He looked in my direction, not seeing me this time, but appeared to be considering climbing back up the stairs. One foot moved to the first step, the other one moved to the second step. Sirens wailed in the distance. He changed his mind, turned and raced for the door.

"No," I shrieked, reminding myself of a banshee as he opened the door.

It slammed shut as I seemed to emit a gust of wind in his direction. I felt sure that Steve's books would have a better name for it though.

Mark swore and opened the door again. The familiar dizziness subdued me and knew I was powerless to do anything else to keep him there until the police arrived.

As I blacked out, I wanted to cry or scream, anything to vent my frustration at how close I came to catching my killer, only to fail at the last hurdle. What if it was my last chance? What if I didn't come back?

Chapter Twelve

I woke up surrounded by darkness, similar to when I first had a vision of the killer.

"Is this it?" I called out. "It can't be," I silently pleaded. After everything; from discovering Paul's sordid secret and protecting my sister from him, to finding the killer and being so close to his capture. If only I made more of an effort, maybe fought to stay for a few more seconds to keep him inside the house until the police got there. All I had to do was fight the dizziness for a few minutes, but I couldn't even do that.

"Welcome back," a voice boomed. It was the same voice as the last time.

"Erm...sorry. What is this place and who are you?" I asked.

"You've been here before."

"Yes, but I didn't know then either."

"This place is where your soul is weighed and judged. It's where your fate is decided. And sometimes, it's where offers are made," the voice responded.

"I don't understand."

"You have seen that your life fell short of what you thought it was. In death, you saved your sister from a doomed relationship and you came closer than you can ever know to catching a killer and saving the countless lives of innocent women."

"I failed," I say, only focussing on the part where I was close, but hadn't succeeded in catching my killer. It was helpful as picking 2, 4, 6, 8, 10 and 12 as my lottery numbers, only for 1, 3, 5, 7, 9 and 11 to be called out.

"You have only failed if you choose to move on now."

I wanted to tell him that I didn't understand again, but stopped myself. He must have thought I was stupid.

"What do you mean?"

That's when he made the offer. I could go back to three days before my death, armed with the knowledge I had gained. My first idea was to save myself, then I understood I could save the other women at the same time.

"You can not save yourself. If you try to and succeed, you will only be brought back here."

"Then what?" I questioned.

"You'll find out." is all he would tell me.

I found his lack of information unhelpful, but he was offering me the chance to go back to my old life, even if it was only for three days. I would be able to talk to the people I cared about and those I no longer cared for, then solve my murder and prevent more murders. Although I still had to die, I shouldn't turn down the rare chance he offered me. The unspoken suggestion of going through my own death again wasn't appealing, but I pushed it to the back of my mind.

"I accept," I said, feeling like I should say something to seal the deal.

He didn't reply, but the darkness was replaced to a small light. It spread until I had to close my eyes to avoid going blind. When I opened them again, I was in my bedroom at Paul's house. He lay next to me on the bed me, sleeping. His arm was slung over my chest, and a smug smile plastered across his face. I batted the invading arm away, more aggressively than I might have if I had woken to a swarm of bees on my chest. At least they have a purpose.

"What?" he yelled, bolting upright, his eyes darting around the room before falling on me as the source of his rude awakening.

"Urgh." I couldn't help myself. I knew I had been sent back to before my murder, which also meant I shouldn't be aware of Paul's fetishes. Having his skin against mine made me want to vomit. So did knowing what he had done and the secret underwear stash he must have tucked away somewhere — soiled with other women's' bodily fluids.

"Stay away from me," I yelled, grabbing a towel from the cupboard to cover myself while I looked around for any of my clothes. I found my underwear in the top drawer; the same one that had been used for my sister's underwear not long after I died. I grabbed a pair of my skinny jeans from the floor and a white t-shirt from the wardrobe. I was dressing as I left the room, hopping along as I put on my jeans, then grabbing at the bannister as my t-shirt went over my head.

"Sarah, what's wrong?" Paul called after me, but didn't attempt to follow.

I picked up my shoes and bag from the bottom of the stairs, then left the house with no notion of where I was going. I walked down the street. A cold wind made my bare arms feel unprotected. I did my best to ignore the cold. It had been so long since the temperature affected me.

"I'm here to stop the killer," I reminded myself. "But not to save myself." Even if I caught pneumonia, it wouldn't finish me off before my three days were up, would it?

"What, dear?" the elderly woman from across the road asked. She stopped walking as her pug came to a halt and did its business on the side of the grass.

"Sorry, nothing. Just reminding myself of what I need to do today."

"Lists, that's what I do. If I write everything down, I can't forget. Unless I lose the list," she added with a laugh.

I forced a smile, but my mind was trying to figure out what I should do first.

"The restaurant," I thought, walking in that direction, checking my bag for my purse and bus pass. Both were there. I changed direction towards the nearest bus stop.

If I waited at The Crusty Edge for long enough, he would probably show up. He must have seen me there before fixating on me.

"Hi, Sarah," Shelly greeted me as I dropped my bag off in my locker at the back of the staffroom upstairs.

"Hi," I said. I only had three days to live, but keeping her talking seemed so important. She was my friend, or the closest person I had to a friend.

"Are you okay?" she asked.

"If I told you something; it's just between us, right?" I asked, looking at my watch and confirming our shift didn't start for another ten minutes.

Shelly looked behind her as if making sure I wasn't talking to someone else. "Of course," she said, after seeing we were the only people in the room.

I began to tell her about Paul and his sordid secret. Emma would never believe me if I told her directly. I thought if I told Shelly, she might spill to Emma after my murder. Despite my lack of female friends, I was aware of the unspoken rule. Women shouldn't sit back and say nothing while a man messed around behind his girlfriend's back. I was relying on her to know about this rule too.

"Are you sure? He seems so into you and not the type to…" she began.

"I followed him to a whorehouse," I said. It's not like I lied. I chose to think of it as omitting the details of when I followed Paul; mainly the fact it hadn't happened yet and I was a ghost at the time.

"Wow," she said, looking at me. 'I guess you can never know someone."

I wanted to talk to her some more, but the clock on the wall turned to 10:01 and we hadn't clocked in.

As I served customers, my eyes kept wandering to the door. If I could talk to him instead of giving him the cold shoulder, maybe he would give me his real name, then I could find a way to let people know who killed me. I thought about the man I talked to inside the darkness. Although, I'm not sure that's the best way to describe the owner of the voice. He never said anything about coming back as a ghost after my second death. I deliberated over whether it would be more permanent. I should have asked, but it all happened so fast and I never expected to be sent back to my old life at all. Lunchtime arrived, and the old couple from before showed up in the middle of the usual rush.

"What can I get you?" I asked, keeping my voice friendly, but making no effort to engage either of them in conversation.

The woman looked at me, then at her husband. I guess she expected the usual annoying chatter, but I was determined to keep talk to a minimum if she hated my yammering so much. She placed an order for the two of them. I don't suppose the poor husband got much choice in what he ate.

"Two bacon rolls, two coffees and a cheesecake," I repeated their order back to them.

"Yes, thank you," the husband confirmed, possibly just to check that his voice box still worked.

"Okay, it won't be long."

"Are you okay?" Shelly asked me as we passed.

"Fine," I replied, my attention already diverting away from her, towards the door.

Mark entered. His eyes met mine. I forced a smile, despite the feeling of my heartbeat increasing. My smile spread, this time because I had a heartbeat. I was alive; the pounding confirmed it. He smiled back, mistaking my grin for joy at seeing him.

"I'll take this one," I muttered to nobody in particular.

I walked towards him, each movement making my legs feel like they were made of lead.

"Hi," I said, forcing enthusiasm into that one word.

I pushed out my chest and twirled with my hair, assuming that's what men like. I'd seen plenty of women flirt that way during their meals and the guys never looked like they objected.

"Hi," he replied.

I brushed my hand lightly against his arm before leading him to the smallest free table, which had room for two diners.

"Is this table okay for you?" I asked.

"Yes, do you want to join me?" he offered, lifting his hand to my arm. It rested there, and I resisted the urge to shrug it off.

"Maybe later. We're so busy. But how about you give me your number and we go somewhere later?"

His eyes widened, but he grinned. Any sign of surprise vanished. He took a pen out of his inside pocket and wrote his number down on the back of a napkin, then handed it to me. I pocketed it, then took his order.

Shelly eyed me as I took the order to the kitchen staff. I pretended not to notice. She caught up with me later while I put my coat on to leave.

"What's going on with you today?" she asked, out of earshot of Paul who was on a later shift, so had only arrived half an hour earlier. I had avoided him the whole time.

"What do you mean?"

"This thing you told me about Paul, and then you start getting cosy and exchanging phone numbers with Mr Handsy?"

"Mr Handsy?"

"The guy who eats here almost every day and mentally undresses the female customers. When it's busy, he uses it as an excuse to brush up against women on the way to the toilet and get a little closer than he needs to. We've had tons of complaints about him."

I couldn't lie to her, not if I wanted us to be friends, even if it would be a short-lived friendship.

"I'm trying to find out who he is, for a friend."

"What friend?"

"He's been bothering someone I know and if I can get his real name, maybe the police can get involved. The name he gave me is Mo." I took out the napkin from my pocket and held it out for her to see.

"Oh," she said, her face creased up.

She probably assumed he was a potential rapist, but the truth was more fatal than that. Both were awful though.

"He told me his name's Mickey, or something like that, but I'm sure I heard him give someone one of the customers a different name," she admitted.

"Exactly, so I need to get cosy with him, as you phrased it. To put myself in a situation where I can sneak a look at his I.D or something with his real name on."

"So, you're going on a date with him?"

I hadn't thought that far ahead, but it seemed like the only way to put myself in a situation where I would learn something important about him.

"I suppose I have to," I said.

"Not without me," she replied.

"You do understand how dating works?" I asked. In truth, I only dated Paul, and watched customers on dates as I took their orders. I was no expert on the technicalities of dating.

"Relax, I'll be discreet. I'll wear a hat and maybe a wig and some clothes I wouldn't normally wear. I'll sit just far enough away so neither of you will recognise me."

I smiled at her. She seemed excited at the prospect of playing spy.

"Why?" I couldn't help asking.

"I moved here from London and didn't know anyone, and you seem like a good person to do this for your friend. I want to be your friend too. Besides, I usually go home and eat a microwave meal for one. Dressing up and spying on your date with Mr Handsy is a definite upgrade to my night."

I wanted to tell Shelly she would be dating James soon and many of those meals for one would soon become meals for two. The thought occurred to me that even if she believed me, it might somehow change things for her. I didn't want to potentially mess things up. So, I kept quiet about her future relationship.

I phoned Mark a.k.a Mr Handsy and arranged a date with him at another restaurant on the other side of the City Centre, where Shelly would be able to watch our every move from a table at the back of the restaurant.

The black wig and fashion glasses combined with a red dress, made it difficult for even me to recognise her at first.

Chapter Thirteen

I sat opposite Mo, as I then started to call him, so he wouldn't realise I knew he used different fake names with me to everyone else.

"Why did you say yes?" He watched me as I considered how to answer the question.

His gaze made me feel like a caged lion who should be free, but instead is made to prowl around the cage, unable to do what comes naturally to it. I was in control of my actions while trying to prise an identity out of Mo, but he was the cage preventing me from doing what I needed to do. I had to find a way to break out and attack him. I pretended to read the menu.

"Sorry?" I asked.

"To the date," his voice grew slightly louder. He was becoming impatient.

"Why not?" I asked.

"Most women say no, and you said you were engaged."

"Did I?"

"Yes. The first time I spoke to you. You don't even remember me, do you?"

"Of course I do. You eat at The Crusty Edge all the time," I waved my hand as if to bat away his suggestion that I didn't remember him.

"Right. So, you remember serving me, but not giving me the brush off the first time I asked you out?"

He was right, but I couldn't admit that to him.

"My fiancé works in the kitchen. I couldn't just…" I twirled a finger around my hair and cast him what I hoped was a shy smile. "But I served you brownies," I guessed.

"So, you really are engaged?" His eyes narrowed. He picked up his fork, his grip tightening around it.

For a second, I thought he might try to lunge across the table and stab me with it. He let go of the fork allowing it to clatter against his wine glass.

"Not anymore." I looked him in the eye, confident that my response fell close enough to the truth. I held up my hands to show I wasn't wearing a ring.

He smiled. If I didn't know better, I would have believed I imagined the earlier reaction. I had to remind myself, this man was a serial killer. He was used to putting on a front to the world one moment, then letting himself go and acting on his psychotic tendencies in the next moment.

"Good." The smile spread across his face making my stomach lurch, but not in a good way.

I looked down at the menu as he explained how much he hated cheaters.

I resisted the urge to tell him how much I hate murderers, especially when one of them is destined to kill me in a few days.

The waiter arrived. After studying the menu, I'd found the smallest main course, two chicken wings with a choice of sides. I opted for a small portion of chips. My appetite had abandoned me. I thought about picking up my fork and stabbing Mo with it. Not only would that stop him killing anyone (including me) it would also make me feel better. I was in a nice restaurant, as a customer instead of a waitress, and able to eat food again. It was only temporary, so I should be enjoying the tastes with the smug knowledge that I no longer had to worry about my weight. Instead, I had to force down every single chip and bite of chicken, as he continued to talk about himself while avoiding giving me anything useful.

"So, I worked at the garage fixing cars," he finished.

I had been looking at him, but my mind wandered elsewhere. It would be useful to discover where he worked, even if he no longer worked there. I doubted he ever worked anywhere near a garage though. Every word coming out of his mouth could be a lie. Chasing up false leads seemed like a good way to squander my limited time.

"Excuse me," I said, standing and using the napkin to wipe away any possible traces of tomato ketchup from my mouth. "I'm going to the toilet, I'll be back in a minute." I left before giving him a chance to say anything else.

Within a minute of sitting down on the toilet, the door squealed, then heals clicked against the floor from outside the cubicle. The owner of the heals let out a small breath.

"Sarah?" Shelly's voice asked.

"Yes, it's me." I finished what I was doing and stepped out of the cubicle.

"Have you got anything useful?" she asked.

"No, just more lies."

"How far are you willing to go with this?" she posed the question that I hadn't wanted to ask myself.

I knew if I went back to his place with him, he would have to go to the bathroom sometime. That would at least give me a minute to look for some I.D or a bill with his real name on. Then I would also know where he lived, unless he had a second address for taking women back to. Something told me the occasion didn't happen often enough for that. I could make my excuses and leave before having to go too far, but what if he didn't need the bathroom until after sex? Could I really let him touch me while knowing he was a killer who preyed on women who spurned him?

"It's okay," Shelly said, seeming to sense my reluctance, or maybe she thought the same way I did. "I have an idea. You should get back to him before he gets suspicious. You've been in here for five minutes."

I left the bathroom first and sat back down on my seat, ignoring the stares from my date.

"What took you so long?"

"Sorry, I had to redo my makeup."

"You look fine." His eyes inspected my face.

I felt like I was being scrutinised. Surely he couldn't be looking for traces of freshly applied make-up. How would he even know whether I re-applied my makeup or not?

"I only wanted to look my best for you," I said softly, curling my finger around a strand of hair again.

He smiled, seeming to accept that.

"So…" he began.

Shelly yelped, grabbing the table as she stumbled, then landed on Mo's lap.

"I am so sorry," she cooed, putting one hand against his chest.

He stared at her. His eyes fell to the mass of black hair. It was a wig, she was still bleach-blonde underneath it at that point. He didn't realise that though. He may have been trying to place where he had seen her before, but the smile he gave her was leering and lustful. His eyes flickered between her hair and generous sized breasts. So, he was a breast man and fond of women with dark hair as well as red. Was this a type, or would he go for blondes too? I tried to figure out who might be his typical victim.

"I didn't hurt you, did I?" Her hand moved down to his trousers brushing against them slightly, but he didn't seem to care. He gasped, clearly enjoying himself. Shelly shot me a look. A satisfied smile flashed across her face just long enough for me to see it. I didn't know what she had done, but I grasped that the date was over. She stood and walked away, looking back only to smile seductively at my leering date.

"That is it," I snapped, impressed at how outraged I sounded. "I am here on a date with you and you practically made out with that woman over the remains of my dinner." I snatched up my coat and bag from the seat next to me and strode towards the exit.

Mo began to stammer a response, but I was already halfway out of the restaurant. I felt the eyes of everyone else drilling into the back of my head, as each one of their owners tried to satisfy their morbid curiosity.

"My wallet," I heard Mo yell as I opened the door, I realised what all the touchy-feely stuff from Shelly had been for. She waited outside for me, grabbing my arm as she laughed and told me to run.

We bolted down the street, but my 4-inch heels slowed me down. I kicked them off and ran barefoot, laughing as Shelly's giggles seemed to be infectious. As we turned the corner, a bus pulled up at the bus shelter a few feet ahead of us. It was heading to Stockport, but that didn't matter. I hadn't planned on returning to Paul's house in Salford Quays anyway.

Neither of us spoke. We jumped on and bought day tickets. The bus pulled away as we took our seats at the back. Mo caught sight of us and chased after the bus. I started to think he might catch up at the next stop. Shelly stood and approached the driver.

"Excuse me," she said. "This guy was chasing me and my friend, even after we told him no and he's chasing the bus now." The driver must have glanced in his rear-view mirror. I couldn't see him from where I sat.

"That guy with the dark hair?"

"Yes, that's him." I stood up and walked to the front of the bus. "He scared me so much, I had to ditch my shoes," I said, lifting one leg for him to look at my barefoot, leaning on Shelly for support as I almost toppled over.

"She had to ditch her shoes," Shelly repeated. "That's how slimy this guy was, wandering hands and eyes, if you get what I mean. Those shoes cost £300."

I looked at Shelly, trying not to smile. I knew there was a reason I wanted to be her friend.

"You must really have wanted to get away from him," the driver exclaimed, before radioing his boss to say he would be missing the next three stops, because two young ladies were being pursued by some creep, his words, not mine, but I didn't disagree.

"Could you call the police as well? So they can keep an eye out for this guy in case he approaches anyone else?" I asked.

***

"You were amazing," I told Shelly after the driver returned us to the city centre on his way back to the depot, even though it wasn't his route and he finished his shift twenty minutes earlier.

"The shoe thing was genius. I never thought to mention that until you did, but it added an extra layer of believability, to the story of us wanting to get away from some handsy creep."

I smiled at her, but part of me wanted to thank her for helping, then tell her I would continue alone. What was I thinking making a new friend a few days before my death?

I didn't tell her I could manage the rest of my plan alone though. Instead, I took her with me to a nearby fast-food restaurant and we went through his wallet.

"His real name is Tim Frey and he lives in Trafford, according to his driving licence." Shelly held it out to me. The picture reminded me of what I imagined his prison photo would look like when the police caught him. All that was missing was the number that prisoners had to hold, if that really happened. I suppose it didn't matter, so long as the prison part happened.

"Thank you," I said. I knew those two words didn't cover everything. I still needed to find a way to ensure that information got to the police after I died, but I had more knowledge about my killer than I did before.

"No problem. That's what friends are for; stealing some creep's wallet to get his personal details." She grinned at me.

"Do you want to come back for a drink to celebrate?" I asked her. I knew Paul would be working late. Afterwards, he would probably go visit his whore.

Shelly didn't reply straight away, and I thought she might say no. I felt relieved when she agreed, because I had an idea how to thank her. Ever since Paul and I got back together after I finished university, I saved every spare pound towards our wedding. It's cringeworthy looking back at it now, to realise I was so needy I saved for our wedding before he even proposed. I had over £1000 in a box at the bottom of the wardrobe, in addition to another thousand in the bank. Paul just assumed the box held more shoes. I would have hoarded more cash if I had pursued a career in journalism, but Paul insisted it was too dangerous.

I let Shelly into the house, listening out for Paul's snores or the sound of him tapping on his laptop in the front room, in case he left work early for whatever reason. I was greeted by silence and a note on the fridge saying there was a problem at the restaurant, so he would be later than usual, and we needed to talk about my earlier outburst.

"The restaurant is closed in an hour, that's when his shift finishes. How can he work later than that?" Shelly asked.

"Exactly," I replied.

"You don't care?"

"I'm past caring," I replied. "I've had time to deal with it."

"I don't think I would be so understanding," she told me.

"I have a present for you," I told her, "to say thanks for your help tonight."

Of course she tried to turn down my gift, saying that's what friends are for – even before she knew what it was. When I presented her with the shoebox full of money, she protested some more.

"This is towards my wedding if that helps," I told her. "It's not happening now."

"Then you keep the money. Use it to go on holiday somewhere. Show that arsehole how you can have fun without him."

"Okay," I agreed, "but hold onto it for me. We'll both go somewhere."

"Really?"

I felt bad lying to her, but that seemed like the only way to get her to take the money with her. Maybe she would remember our conversation and take a holiday after my murder.

Chapter Fourteen

I called in sick the following day. Graham threatened to fire me if I didn't return the next morning with a sick note from my doctor. Obviously, his words didn't bother me. I was on day two of my brief return; the following night I would be murdered. Getting fired didn't quite make it to the list of things concerning me anymore.

I had slept in the spare room. I didn't know or care what Paul thought about that. He was still sleeping after 10am, probably exhausted from his sordid antics. I let him sleep while I packed. As I squeezed a t-shirt into the bag, I looked around at everything I always thought I needed. The television attached to the wall of the bedroom had barely been used in the two years since we purchased it. I recalled giving Paul all my reasons for why we needed a 40-inch television in the bedroom, rather than the small portable TV/DVD combi we owned before that.

"We can spend weekends snuggled up in bed watching TV when we're snowed in," my voice seemed to echo back at me from years earlier.

In reality, we spent one weekend in bed after four inches of snow made it too cold for us to venture outside. By the next time it snowed, Paul had invested in snow boots and he walked to the restaurant, saying that he had to keep the place open or customers would go somewhere else. I don't know why he felt like it was down to him.

The king-sized bed where Paul sprawled out was his idea. He convinced me we needed it, insisting it would spice up our love life and help us to sleep better. Maybe he was right, but he began spicing up his own sex life without me or the king-sized bed. My only regret when it came to my relationship with Paul was wasting so much of my life on him. I could have been with someone else, or just making friends with women like Shelly, women who would have my back. Looking back, I didn't have much to be happy or proud of in my life. I thought I was happy with Paul, but I wouldn't be able to explain why if anyone ever asked me how my life with Paul made me happy.

I picked up the bag and left the room, the house, my life. I kept walking until I reached my mum's house.

"Sarah?" she asked.

I assumed she was surprised to see me, rather than needing to question whether it was me. I didn't visit often, but my visits weren't so infrequent that she could forget what I looked like.

"I left Paul. Can I come in?" I asked.

Mum gaped at me while opening the door wider, then she stepped aside to let me pass.

"What happened?" she asked.

"He prefers kinky prostitutes, but that's not why I'm here," I said, unable to resist mentioning Paul's indiscretion, sure that my mum wouldn't be able to stop herself from mentioning something like that to Emma after my death.

"What?"

"Can we not talk about it right now?"

"Okay. Are you…staying?" the last word was full of more surprise.

I couldn't blame my mum for her astonishment or confusion. As soon as I got the opportunity to move out, I did. Afterwards, I only visited on special occasions or when I needed something.

"Just think of it as you repaying me for all the time I lost with Dad," I recalled saying after she accused me of using her.

"When will I be up to date with my payments?" she asked.

"Never," I told her.

I can't figure out why she never told me to get lost after the way I treated her.

I forced myself back to the present moment, realising if I wanted answers to my questions, I would have to apologise first. More importantly, telling my mum how sorry I felt was the right thing to do.

"I'm sorry," I said.

"For what?" Her response could have been sarcastic, asking which of all the things I ever did or said, I was apologising for. It sounded like a genuine question though.

"I treated you like…I don't know exactly, but you never sent me away and I still treated you like shit."

My mother took a step back, her eyes scrunched together, looking at me as though waiting for the punch line.

"I'm sorry," I said again.

"You're my daughter. I've always done my best for you, or at least what I thought was best. I could have been wrong though."

"I just don't understand why you stopped me from seeing Dad, but I'm sure you had your reasons?"

"Your dad…" she began.

'What?'

"Your dad is one of those situations where I thought I was doing the right thing. I always meant to tell you the truth when you were older, but I…"

"The truth?" I asked, studying my mum's serious expression as a tear leaked out.

Was she fake crying again? If so, she had gotten better at it. No, it was real. She turned away, dabbing her fingers against her face to prevent me from seeing.

"Dad didn't die of cancer?" I asked, but I already had the nagging voice in my head telling me I was right.

"You were his favourite. I know parents aren't meant to have favourites, but I'm sure it's because you were so like him in some ways. That's why you understood each other. He was hot-headed and outgoing to the point where people less outgoing felt a little overwhelmed in his presence."

"I came here to apologise, but I'm glad you're being honest with me. So, what happened?"

"Sorry, Sarah. I'm just a little taken aback. I don't recall you ever apologising to me before. You were young and I couldn't tell you the truth because you looked up to him. So, I had to lie to you, then to your sister to stop you from finding out the truth. He ran off with his secretary. All those visits to the hospital. That was me going to his workplace and trying to convince him to come home. Not for me; I couldn't have gone back to how things were before he cheated. But for you girls, especially you, Sarah. You needed him in your life."

I looked at her, wondering if she would have stayed with my dad if he returned home. I imagined how awkward the relationship between them would have been. She no longer loved him, just like I no longer loved Paul.

"I'm glad he didn't come back," I said, pushing aside the realisation of how we both fell for the wrong men.

"You never seemed glad. The way you used to yell at me and tell me how I kept you away from him, it sounded like you wished I was dead." The tears were rolling down her face now. She no longer seemed able to keep up the pretence of not crying by dabbing her face. She had given up and allowed them to ruin her perfectly applied make-up.

"If you told me the truth, I would have dealt with it. I might be a better daughter," I told her. Tears streamed down my face too. They were wet and stung my eyes, proving themselves to be real, not like the ghost tears I had only been able to imagine like a phantom limb.

"It's not too late," my mother said through a small smile.

The hope in her words and her expression only made me cry more. Of course, she didn't know this was my last full day. She didn't realise I would sleep at her house that night if she let me, but the following night my body would be lying lifeless in an alley in the middle of town for the second time. How could she know? If I told her, she wouldn't believe me. Even if she did, she would try to keep me at her house, refuse to let me go out to meet my death. There was no way she would understand that it had to happen. I struggled to find the words to explain it, but if I wanted to stop Tim from killing all the women he murdered after me, I needed to die in a way that would lead the police to him. If I managed to escape my fate, it would be the most selfish thing I had ever done and from the sound of things, I would die anyway. I might as well have it mean something. I was at Mum's to make up for the way I treated her and hopefully to be a better sister to Emma, by giving my mum the gossip about Paul. I wanted to stop being so selfish. Letting Tim kill me would be the final step in doing the right thing in my life.

"No, it's not too late," I agreed with my mum, omitting the fact that it was almost too late.

"Let me make some of that lemonade you used to like," she exclaimed.

"You haven't made lemonade in years."

"Your fourteenth birthday. I wondered why you hadn't drunk any of it. That was until I found you behind the shed at the bottom of the garden, drinking cider."

"That stuff tasted disgusting," I recalled.

"No wonder, you bought the shops own brand and double strength too. I remember you throwing up after I made you eat the chicken dinner I cooked. I knew eating so much food after drinking all that awful cider would make you sick."

"Then why make me eat it?" I asked, unable to stop myself from grinning.

"It taught you a lesson, didn't it? I don't recall you drinking alcohol for a few years after that."

"Good point." I didn't have the heart to tell her how I saved up my pocket money for months at a time to buy better brands.

We sat and talked until lunchtime, before mum asked if I was going into work.

"No, not today. I'll be back there tomorrow though." My eyes wandered around the room. I didn't notice anything to suggest she was going to move in with Martin in the very near future. No photos of them together; no items accidently left behind from his overnight stays. Even a trip to the bathroom didn't result in me finding so much as a spare toothbrush. They had to be seeing each other though. Things couldn't escalate from dating to moving in together so soon after my death otherwise.

"It's okay if you're seeing someone," I said to Mum as we sat on the sofa, watching some old murder mystery. I didn't understand why the woman ran around the house locking all the doors after hearing a noise from upstairs. The would-be killer was clearly already in the house with her.

"Who would I see?" my mother feigned ignorance.

I guess she expected me to go back to my old self and have a go at her if she mentioned Martin to me.

"Martin, maybe. He's single and he seems to like you."

"Where are you getting this from?" Her face flushed as she tried to cover her left cheek with her hand.

"I think he might be good for you, that's all," I said.

"I'll keep that in mind," she said between forced laughs.

"Good." At least she knew I was okay with her relationship. "I made a new friend at work. Her name is Shelly," I offered the information, changing the subject for her benefit.

"Really?"

"Well don't act so surprised. I'm not that horrible, am I?"

"Of course not. You have your moments. I don't recall you ever having a female friend who wasn't just dating one of your boyfriend's mates."

"I didn't have that many boyfriends," I protested. The truth is, Paul remained the only boyfriend I had in my reduced life — though because I hung around with his friends, people assumed I had gone through lots of relationships. I understood what she meant though. I thought the same thing about my lack of female friends. That's why, when faced with the prospect of no longer being alive, I took the selfish option and befriended Shelly. I didn't want to be remembered as the woman with no real friends.

I thought about Steve. He was a friend too. He wasn't female though. I found myself realising, the person I had become could easily develop feelings for him. He had flaws, but so did I. We were both struggling to be better though.

"I need to go out for a few hours," I told my mum.

"You're not taking him back, not after the prostitutes!" she exclaimed.

"What? No, I'm going to see my friend."

"Shelly?"

"No, another new friend, Steve."

"Wow. You have been busy," she retorted.

"You don't know the half of it," I muttered as I reached the hallway and was safely out of earshot.

Chapter Fifteen

I hung around outside Steve's front door.

This was a bad idea? What was I going to say? I had done one selfish thing in making friends with Shelly. Would I make that two by messing up Steve's life as well? Granted, it was already a mess, but what improvement could I make to it in under twenty-four hours?

I turned to leave, but the words "twenty-four hours" seemed to bounce around inside my head. That wasn't long enough for me to grow on him. It took weeks for him to start thinking of me as a friend, rather than an annoying ghost. Maybe I could help him though. I banged on the door before giving myself a chance to back out.

"Can I help you?" Steve asked, peering out from behind the door. His hair looked like one of those hair gel advertisements gone wrong. It had a unique style, but it wasn't one which anyone would want to emulate.

"You need to sort yourself out," I said, wishing I had at least taken the time to prepare what I wanted to say to him.

"Excuse me?"

I didn't blame him for the indignance in his voice. It's not the done thing to knock on a stranger's door and demand they sort their life out, even if they do in fact need to sort their life out.

"So what if you didn't complete your journalism degree? You're a damn good freelance journalist and if you cleaned up your house a little more, tidied up your appearance and got out there to go after the kind of stories where you interact with large groups of people, you would feel less cluttered and weighed down and less alone. And you know what else? We all feel alone sometimes. So what if you're more alone than other people because you see ghosts and they don't? And so what if you have to hide that part of yourself from people? We've all got something that makes us different; something that people would be put off by. This is 2020 though and at least people are more open to ghosts and paranormal activity. If this was hundreds of years ago, you might be burnt as a witch. Just think about that the next time you're feeling sorry for yourself." I finally stopped talking, aware that he was staring at me. His mouth opened, but he stayed silent, as if all the words had been taken away.

"Who are you?" he managed to say.

"A friend," I said, before I turned and left him on his doorstep to contemplate the words of a seemingly mad woman who he didn't know, despite me knowing things I couldn't know about him. Even then, I understood I missed the chance to really get to know him, because of how self-absorbed I was when I discovered he was the only one with the ability to see me.

I returned to my mum's house for the night. I could have gone to see Emma, but there was nothing more for me to do to warn her off Paul, and nothing profound enough to change all the years we wasted while drifting apart.

I stared at the ceiling while trying to get to sleep in my old room. There was a small double bed and a chest of drawers in the room, but my mind drifted to a time when two single beds, two chests of drawers and a wardrobe all made the room seem more cramped. I always felt like we constantly fought for space as Emma tried to sneak her clothes into my drawers or my side of the wardrobe. I closed my eyes, seeing the images in my mind. Me and Emma arguing over space (or clothes) such as her borrowing my clothes and never returning them. The night I thought Dad died was different though.

I drifted off to sleep and dreamt of that night.

"Your dad passed away in hospital. His body became too weak to fight the cancer any longer," Mum said. The lack of tears at the time made me assume I shouldn't cry either. I needed to be strong for Emma. Mum cried later, enough for the three of us. I held my sister's hand, something I rarely did. She called out for Dad; of course she did. Even in the dream and armed with the knowledge that Dad was still alive, I wanted to cry.

"Where did he go?" became Emma's catchphrase for months.

I had no answer for her.

"Heaven, the next life, somewhere else," I threw random ideas at her. I couldn't change the dream to tell her that he might be watching over her; or at least he might if he was actually dead.

I woke up with the urge to punch the wall? Dad was alive. Would I rather he was dead? Of course not. I even understood why Mum lied and how she had to keep up the pretence.

"You can't miss school, not with exams coming," she told me when I pleaded to go to the funeral. She even stood in the kitchen wearing a black dress when I returned home from school.

"It was just a quiet sermon before the cremation. He wouldn't have wanted a fuss," she told me when I asked.

I wanted a big fuss over my life about to be cut short. I wanted dramatic tear-jerking songs and wailing like in some other cultures. Afterwards though, I wanted people to move on – with the exception of Tim. I wanted him to rot in jail for the rest of his life, which I hoped would be short but miserable. If television was to be believed, he'd become someone's bitch soon enough.

Maybe the things I wanted were selfish. I started to change after the day I found myself standing in the morgue next to my dead body, but it was subtle rather than an unrecognisable transformation. I still hoped for public outpourings of grief from time to time. It's only natural to want people to miss you after you're gone.

I got up and dressed shortly after 6am. It was just getting light out, signalling the beginning of autumn when mornings would become lighter later and darkness would arrive sooner in the evenings. It would be dark when I died, I acknowledged. The acceptance which washed over me, gave me a strange kind of peace I'd never be able to explain — unless the person I was talking to also had inside knowledge of how their own life would reach an abrupt end.

Before leaving my mum's house I placed Tim's I.D under the pillow on my bed, then put my makeup bag into my rucksack. I hoped my mum would find the driving licence later; and the lipstick in my makeup bag could be used to write the name of my killer.

I ran all the way to Emma's flat, even though she lived over two miles away from Mum — and I've never been athletic. There was no mirror, but I imagined my face close to a shade of purple. The wheezing sound in my throat and nostrils must have made me sound even closer to death than I already was.

Emma answered the door, muttering something. Her hair was dishevelled, and her face unusually make-up free. Despite our lack of closeness over the years, I thought I saw concern flash across her face.

"Sarah, what's wrong?" she asked, beckoning me inside and shutting the door behind us.

The way she locked the door; using a top and bottom bolt, one key, a Yale lock and a chain made me wonder what she was so afraid of, to make her go to so much trouble securing her door. Urmston didn't have a high enough crime rate to warrant all those security measures. She wanted to keep someone out, but who?

"I…I just needed to talk to you." I was finally there and I had no idea what I should say.

"It's not even 7am," she replied. She lifted her hand to her hair and I saw bracelet with a heart shaped charm as the sleeve of her robe slid down her arm to reveal her wrist. Paul bought it for my twenty-first birthday. I recalled taking it off before bed as I always did, a few months before my murder. When I woke up the next morning, it was nowhere to be seen.

I pushed that realisation to the back of my mind. The bracelet wasn't why I was there. I already knew Emma and Paul went behind my back. Him stealing back the bracelet he bought me, so he could give it to Emma didn't register as newsworthy in the grand scheme of things.

"This is going to sound strange, but…" I began, trying to find the right words.

"Go on," she urged.

"I'm sorry we weren't closer, like sisters should be."

"You're right, that is strange. You apologising to me."

"I've been thinking a lot about this. If something happened to me, I wouldn't want things with us to be the way they are now."

"Are you dying," she asked. Her expression was unreadable. I couldn't tell if the idea of me dying made her feel worried, or if the prospect didn't concern her either way.

"No, I mean yes. Maybe."

"Well, which is it?"

"Aren't we all dying from the moment we're born?" I asked, realising how naff the words sounded, even while I was still speaking them.

"You woke me up for this?" she snapped, turning back to the door.

She was going to kick me out if I didn't say anything else. I didn't want the last time she saw me to be her telling me to leave her flat.

"I'm sorry for my part in how things never worked out between us, and I want you to know I forgive you for your part. Just…"

"Just what?" She began unlocking the door.

"Paul was never a good choice for either of us."

She turned the key, glaring at me. Her eyes only looked away long enough to turn the Yale lock and slide the chain open.

"Out, I don't know what this is, but I'm too tired for it and I've got a lot to sort out today."

"It's okay," I said, resting my hand on her free arm as she used her other hand to pull the door open. "Really, it's okay." The last thing I wanted was for her to look back at this and feel guilty for turning me away just hours before my brutal murder. "You couldn't have done anything to change things. Remember that."

She rolled her eyes. "Whatever," she snapped.

I told myself, Emma had no way of understanding what I was talking about, or what was would happen later that day.

As I walked away, I heard beeps from behind her door as though she was setting an alarm system. It was my turn to roll my eyes. Nobody was getting past all those locks. The alarm was unnecessary.

Before going to work, I found the alley where I felt sure I was murdered. It wasn't easy with so many alleys everywhere I went. Were they always so many? Maybe I just noticed them more. I used the lipstick and wrote Tim in enormous letters beside the bin near where I had seen my dying body left behind, during the recollection of my own murder

When I arrived at work later that morning, the stony expression on my manager's face looked even more unwelcoming than my sister kicking me out of her flat at 7am.

"You decided to show up for work then? Well done you."

"Sorry, I was ill yesterday."

"I don't care what problems you and Paul might have, but it doesn't affect work, unless you no longer want to work here."

"Yes, sorry." I said.

His expression changed slightly. I'm guessing he expected an argument, or for me to plead with him or try to explain my absence. It seemed pointless to try any of those tactics though.

"Get to work," he barked at me.

The only reason I didn't tell him to stick his job was I assumed I should do things the same as the first time around, or as much as I could. I had deviated enough.

I found Shelly standing by the lockers.

"Tim came in here yesterday looking for you. I thought he might have recognised me, but I don't think he did. He's not happy with you though."

I shrugged, but I hadn't thought about seeing Tim again until the evening. I realised I might have to deal with him sooner.

He showed up at Lunchtime. I couldn't go to the kitchen to avoid him, because I was already avoiding Paul who wanted me to tell him why I hadn't come home the previous night.

"You stole my wallet," Tim hissed at me, grabbing my arm. His fingers dug into my flesh.

"I didn't." I tried without success to pull my arm away.

"Don't be smart with me. Your friend groped me as a distraction and you both ran off with my wallet."

"I don't know what you're talking about." I looked at him, hoping my expression conveyed confusion.

"Tell me who the other one is and I'll go easy on you."

"Are you threatening me?"

"No. Like you said, you didn't steal it. She did."

"It was just me," I found myself saying.

"Are you sure that's your final answer?" He stared at me as if challenging me not to change my mind.

"That's my final answer," I confirmed, doing my best to out-stare him.

"Okay, your funeral."

I walked away, knowing how right he was.

Chapter Sixteen

I walked home alone that night, after brushing off Paul's request to talk later. He even offered me a lift home — if I waited for two hours after my shift, but I refused. The temptation was there. I don't think there's anyone who wouldn't be tempted to wait for a lift from their cheating partner in order to avoid meeting their fate at the hands of a serial killer.

I wanted to live. I wanted to go on holiday with Shelly; to post pictures of us drunkenly falling into swimming pools and being stupid. I imagined myself joining some kind of group, possibly drama and acting in a stage play while my mum watched from the audience. Maybe my sister would show up to watch too.

I saw the scene play out in my head of the life I never had, or never would have. Emma arrived for the after party of the opening night, even though it was only a local production. She held onto the arm of a hot blonde guy. His smile was genuine as Emma introduced him to

Mum and me. I could tell that he wouldn't cheat, and I felt happy for my sister.

"You were great," my mum would tell me, with pride in her voice for the first time I could recall in a long time.

I was jolted out of my imaginary future by footsteps behind me. I knew without having to turn around, it was Tim. The street lights flickered a little. Even though my memories of this night the first time around remained incomplete, I was sure that didn't happen before. I took it as a sign from whatever powers that be, that I shouldn't try to avoid what was about to happen — because it would play out to the same conclusion one way or another.

I worked hard in the previous few days to leave my life better than the first time around. I didn't want to risk all of that being undone. I refused to believe my death would be the end. It couldn't be. Even if I hadn't become a ghost the first time I was killed, I might still cling to the hope that there had to be something more afterwards.

I turned to face Tim.

"This way," I said.

He looked at me surprised, before I quickened my pace and headed for the alley where I would die. I was within a stone's throw of the cinema, but nobody cared or was sober enough to notice as they staggered out of the nearby bars. I reached it as he grabbed a chunk of my hair pulling me backwards. I almost toppled over. The empty car parked on the curb steadied me and my right hand rested on it. I used my left hand to pull my hair from his grip. He let go, taking a handful of hair with him. From the stinging in my scalp, it felt like he might have taken some of that too.

I ran halfway down the alley before he caught up with me. It was no surprise when I twisted my neck and saw the glint of the knife, but I still yelped in anticipation of the pain I was about to feel.

I turn to stare at him in a final act of defiance.

He screwed his face up. "Beg for your life, bitch," he hissed.

I continued to stare until the sharp blade was pressed to my throat. I backed away half a step. His fingers clamped around my arm, preventing me from moving further away.

"Do it; just know I'll be the last." I couldn't resist having one final dig at him.

"What's that supposed to mean?" he snapped, letting go of my arm and punching me hard in my gut.

I keeled over. A light shone down the alley from the car parked at the end, as the owner prepared to drive away – unaware of what was taking place not far from him or her. I could have screamed. The driver would hear if I screamed loud enough. Then what? Maybe it was some elderly woman? She wouldn't be much help and I'd probably be getting her killed too. My eyes shot over to where I had written Tim's name. I wanted to be sure I died close enough to it that it would cause the police to see a possible link, especially after the driving licence was discovered in my old room at Mum's house.

Instead of the bright red lipstick spelling out my killer's name, there was a fresh coat of white paint covering all the graffiti, including my own contribution.

"No," I gasped. If I died right there, I would only have the I.D in my old bedroom to rely on as evidence. That could be anything, like some bloke I had a one-night stand with, even though I never would. It might not be enough for the police to be suspicious and link Tim to my murder.

I was still on the floor as Tim approached me. The car engine started. Within seconds the owner would drive away. I grabbed Tim between the legs, squeezing and twisting hard as I let out a blood-curdling scream, drowning out his grunts of pain.

The car drove away. Either the driver didn't hear, or didn't want to get involved.

"Bitch," he squealed, almost like a girl.

My sense of accomplishment was short-lived. Searing pain shot through my hand and up to my wrist, forcing me to let go. The warm sticky substance, which I belatedly grasped was my own blood, provided an odd source of comfort to me. That's why I didn't use my good hand to stop his leg as he booted me in the face. I fell back, landing in something wet, probably a puddle, maybe somebody's piss though. I really hoped I wasn't going to die in some stranger's piss, not that it made it any better if I knew who it belonged to. Looking back, it must have been the loss of blood making me think that way. I should have felt more concerned about the act of dying itself than the logistics.

"You're the first. Thank you for making this happen," the sicko said to me. He straddled me, grinding against me, even though both of us were still fully clothed. "I'm not going to implicate myself by doing…anything, but I can't tell you how good this feels. The headlight from a passing car briefly illuminated part of his face to show that his mouth was open. He made panting sounds, like he was close to orgasm.

"Just kill me," I snapped. I didn't have the energy to fight. Those words took up most of my energy, but I preferred death over the weird sexual excitement he seemed to be get from my near dead body. I wanted it all to be over.

"I want to savour this," he whispered.

He groped my right breast through my blouse, gasping for breath as if he was the one dying. That's when I realised he wore gloves like the ones you might use for cleaning or washing up.

A siren wailed from somewhere I couldn't identify. Not close enough to save me, I grasped, but enough to make Tim roll off me.

"Sorry to cut this short." His tone gave away his disappointment.

I screamed as I felt the knife plunge into my stomach. Despite the pain, I thought about the piñata at a birthday party. I didn't remember whether it was mine or Emma's. It didn't matter, but I felt like the piñata lying there in the alley. The difference was, instead of sweeties pouring out of me, I had blood rushing out of my stomach and wrist.

Blood, I thought. I saw little of anything from where I lay, but I managed to roll over to the industrial size bin. I lifted my bleeding wrist, rubbing against the bin, despite the pain. My open wounds scraping against the ground and the bin caused me to wince as I scrawled what I hoped was a T, then an I, followed by an M. I couldn't see my handiwork clearly enough to confirm anything. I closed my eyes as I heard a car pull up nearby and footsteps approaching, closer and closer. I knew they were too late, even as a woman's voice said something. I failed to make out the words. She sounded like she moved further away the more she spoke to me.

I envisioned someone with the same reassuring tone of voice, speaking incoherently, while I reversed into a tunnel, leaving her at the opening. Her face was obscured by unnatural daylight as I continued moving like I had become a train, before I became completely immersed in darkness.

"Welcome back," a familiar voice greeted me.

"I have to go back. I can't...I don't know if I planted enough evidence for them to find my killer."

"You did a good job," the voice responded. He sounded calm and authoritative in contrast to everything I felt.

"Does that mean they got the bast...does that mean they got him?" I wasn't sure I should swear in front of him. It seemed like swearing at God. I didn't want him to send me to hell.

"They haven't caught the bastard yet." His use of the word caught me off-guard. "but I trust you can change that, if you so desire."

I wanted to argue that I was dead. How could I change anything now? A surge of light lit up the whole of wherever I was, before I had time to say anything. I had to close my eyes.

When I reopened them, I was standing in the morgue again. My dead body on the slab made me take a step back, even though I had seen it before. This time it had different injuries; a bruised face from where Tim kicked me, the cut hands leading all the way to my slit open wrist – which had dried up, and a larger wound across my stomach.

"Why am I here?" I yelled, my voice sounding like it was somewhere else.

"You still have work to do, think of this as a test," the same voice from earlier whispered, but I couldn't see anyone or place the location of the voice, other than it seemed to be everywhere at once,

"A test for what? I'm dead."

Silence greeted me. I waited, but still received no response. I heard voices though.

"You stay the fuck away from her," my mum's voice yelled.

She flung the door open as she entered, closely followed by Paul. His face was red, his lips trembled. I tried to distinguish whether he was angry or about to cry, but I no longer knew him, if I ever did.

"She's my fiancée," he announced.

Hearing him say the word "fiancée" had no impact on me, other than to make me question my own judgement.

"You should have considered that before you shacked up with those whores," Mum snapped.

Paul's face drained of colour. "How… I mean, what?"

"She told me. In fact, how do I know you aren't the one who did this to her?" she demanded.

"I didn't, I wouldn't," Paul said.

My mum was no longer listening. Her eyes washed over my dead body. She shrieked, then sobbed. A man in a long white overall hurried into the room.

"You should have at least covered her," Paul snapped at him.

"Of course, but I thought you were here to see her." The man looked from Paul to my mum.

"I am," my mum said. "I'm her mother, but this man should not be here. Sarah left him. He could even be a murder suspect. Surely he shouldn't be permitted near the body." She broke into uncontrollable sobs.

The man hurried back to the door. I heard him saying something to whoever waited out there. Two policemen entered the room and steered Paul away.

"We'll need to speak to you, sir," one of them said. "Either here, or at the station."

I stayed with my mum as she held the hand of the body which used to be mine. It had become an empty shell now, but she talked to it like I was still in there, rather than standing unseen behind her.

"Did he do this to you?" she asked.

"No, it was Tim. You need to look in my bedroom, Mum" I couldn't help replying, despite knowing she wouldn't hear. I would need to adjust to being dead all over again.

"I should have protected you," she said.

"Nothing you could do would have stopped this, but you can do something now. You can find the Identification in my room. His name and address are on it."

She turned around, her eyes in my direction, but then shook her head and left. For a moment, I almost allowed myself to hope she heard me. I followed her into the corridor. She passed Paul, where he spoke to the two policemen in hushed tones.

"I didn't hurt her," Paul hissed.

"Don't believe a word that comes out of his cheating mouth," Mum said. "He's been visiting whores. He probably wanted my daughter out of the way after she found out."

I had never seen my mum defend me so fiercely before. I suppose I never gave her reason to after the way

I treated her. Unfortunately, she was pointing the finger at the wrong person. If the police became so focussed on Paul as the main suspect, by the time they concluded he was innocent of murder, it might be too late for someone else.

Chapter Seventeen

I knew if I showed up at Steve's house, he would help me sooner or later, especially if I was nicer to him than my first time as a ghost. Although, I worried that things might play out the same way as before – with him ending up in a cell, accused of my murder. I didn't want to risk it.

I went to my mum's house instead. Emma was there, but she was being strong by comforting Mum as she wept in between rants about Paul and his whores.

The information I gave my mum in order to help Emma, worked too well. Now he'd become the prime suspect as far as she was concerned. On the bright side, Emma looked disgusted at the idea of Paul seeing prostitutes. I even caught her searching on her phone for a nearby sexual health clinic. Just because I didn't want her to be with a cheat, that didn't mean I had forgiven her. Her anxiety over the possibility of having caught something, provided enough satisfaction for me though.

As I considered reintroducing myself to Steve, I noticed my sister kept moving her eyes around the room whenever my mum's attention was diverted away from her. What was she looking for? I told myself it didn't matter, but I continued to spy on her. Emma's mobile buzzed in her pocket. The vibrating sound resembled a small drill. It must have gone off at least ten times. I saw her jolt in her seat each time. It was obvious she was aware of someone trying to get hold of her, but she ignored it. I told myself it was out of respect to Mum. She couldn't be texting or answering calls to her friends when Mum grieved over me.

The digital clock on the mantelpiece read 02:37 am, when mum fell asleep. Her eyes flickered. She let out small snores, in between mumbling something I didn't understand. Emma didn't seem able to decipher her words either. My sister shrugged to herself, while shifting in the sofa and allowing Mum to lie down a little more until Emma was off the sofa and Mum was lying flat.

Emma stood, looking down at Mum for a few minutes. Her eyes darted around the room, then back to Mum.

"What are you up to?" I whispered, in case Mum was in a sleep state where she might hear me. There was something more going on than my sister waiting for an appointment at a sexual health clinic.

She shivered, even though the thermometer on the wall showed that it was 15c, so hardly shivering temperature. I had witnessed Emma go outside in colder climates, wearing next to nothing. I followed her up the stairs. When she reached the landing, she took out her mobile and dialled a number I didn't recognise. It was listed under Joan. I never heard her mention anyone called Joan, but that meant very little. I didn't know who any of her friends were.

"I'm in the house now," she said.

She paused while the other person spoke.

"I'm about to. If it's anywhere, it'll be in her room," Sarah whispered.

Another pause.

"Okay, I'll call you if I find it."

What was she looking for? I asked myself. This didn't feel right. I did my best to ignore the nagging voices in the back of my head, not wanting to believe any of the things they suggested. I followed her into my bedroom.

It wasn't the way I would usually leave it. The bed remained unmade after my haste to get to Emma's and make up for years of us being distant. I should have known a few minutes would never solve the issues between us. I had to try though, or I thought so at the time.

Emma went to the chest of drawers, rifling through my underwear before searching the other drawers where I didn't have much. Everything was still at Paul's. I only packed one bag when I left him. That's all I needed.

"What are you looking for?" I asked.

Emma let out a loud sigh, then swore under her breath.

She looked lost as she glanced around the bedroom, even though we had shared the room as children. She knelt on all fours, twisting her head to search under the bed.

By this point I became annoyed. Was she looking for something of mine to steal now that I was dead? I recalled her borrowing my clothes without permission. On the few occasions she returned them, it was after they were stained or damaged. This was a new low, I mused. It made no sense though. Why would she need to phone someone about stealing her dead sister's belongings?

She took in deep breaths, struck the floor with both hands, then pulled herself to her feet. Emma stood for a few moments, muttering something too quietly for me to make out the words, then threw herself onto the bed. Her hands slapped against the mattress. She punched one of my pillows. I couldn't tell if this was what she wanted to do to me, or if it was a strange form of mourning for the sister she never really had. Did she suddenly regret all the times we could have been there for each other? I stepped forward – wanting to reach out, close to sympathy for my younger sibling before her next actions shattered those feelings, like delicate crystals dropping from a great height.

One of the pillows toppled onto the floor. She picked up the other one and flung it against the wall.

I saw the driving licence before she did, remembering I wanted my mum or the police to find it. I stared at my sister, hoping she would look down and at least care enough to tell the police about the identification she found in my room. Even if she had to come up with a cover story about what she was doing in my room, she'd tell them. Wouldn't she? Emma must have the sense to grasp how it could be linked to my murder.

Her gaze fell to the licence. Tim's eyes stared straight ahead. I understand that passports and driving licence pictures make most people look like suspects from a most wanted list, but his would have made the top ten. It screamed dangerous serial killer with a side-serving of serious fetish for women close to death. The image of him dry humping me as I bled out, invaded my memories.

"Sicko," I muttered, shaking my head in an attempt to shake off the memory.

"Got you," Emma exclaimed, picking up the evidence needed to navigate the police's spotlight onto my killer.

"Take it to the police," I urged, knowing she couldn't hear, but the suggestion might somehow reach her without her knowing it was mine.

Instead, she shoved it into her back-left pocket and took out her phone from her front pocket. She dialled the same number as before.

"I got it," she said. "I'll bring it straight to you."

There was a pause.

"Yes, and the money too. Then we're square and I never see you again, do you hear me?"

She hung up without waiting for a response.

I wanted to scream at her; to lash out and hit her or take away something she cared about. Anything just to hurt her a fraction of the way her actions had done to me. She killed me – not with her own hands – but she had killed me. Instead of trying any of the things I wanted to do to her, I stood there staring at her. Even with my scrambled thoughts, I understood she was calling Tim, not Joan. She had stolen the evidence against him and was paying him for killing me. When I went to see her and she said she had a lot of things to do, I never suspected one of the things on her to-do list was making final arrangements for my murder. I didn't want to believe it though.

That's why I followed her, hoping for another explanation; anything at all to prove myself wrong. As distant as we were when I was alive, I wanted to be wrong about this.

Emma caught a taxi to an address in Sale, the same one on Tim's driving license. I told myself there must be another reason for her being there. Maybe it was a setup to catch my killer, but that didn't add up either.

When she stood on his doorstep, I watched unseen by her side, hoping the address was wrong and someone else lived here – no matter how much of a coincidence that would be.

"Get inside," Tim hissed, opening the door wider and pulling my sister over the doorstep by her arm.

I followed her inside. Walking through the closed door reminded me I was dead again, permanently this time, I assumed.

"Here." She shoved the I.D into his hand, turning to leave as Tim tried to turn the Yale lock.

Emma batted his hand away, turning the locked the other way to open the door.

"Wait," he persisted, putting his hand over hers and pressing his body against her. He was only wearing a dressing gown; it fell open a little. He looked down at the same time Emma did.

My sister crumpled up her face, even more than the time I gave her a bag of sour drops to eat and she poured half the bag into her mouth without knowing what they were.

That made me laugh. I wasn't laughing this time though.

"Get out," I snapped at Emma, temporarily forgetting she had just handed over an important piece of evidence in my murder case.

"Let me go," she said, her voice faltering.

"Pay me, it doesn't have to be money," he said, his lips moved closer to her neck.

She shuddered, pushing him away with one hand and reaching into her bag with the other. She pulled out what can't have been more than £3000, then shoved the bundle of notes into his hands.

"That's all my life is worth?" I snapped.

I looked at her, waiting for an explanation. None arrived. Of course, she didn't know I was there.

We weren't close, I told myself, but it wasn't enough to excuse her. Plenty of families aren't close. Not everyone pays some creepy weirdo to kill their sibling though.

"You don't have to leave," Tim persisted, grabbing at Emma as she unlocked the door – managing to pull it halfway open before he tried to stop her. For a second, I considered letting him do the same thing to her as he did to me. I saw the gleam in his eye. He was like a wild animal, brought up to be tame before getting its first taste of blood. I could tell he was hooked. I was the first, but he would kill again. He got off on it in the most sexually perverse way. Emma would be his second. I thought of Mum. I imagined her getting the call; her second, and only remaining daughter killed in the same way as her oldest. It would destroy her. I had read about people overcome by grief not living much longer after so much loss. Maybe it was the stress, but I couldn't let Emma die, for Mum's sake if no other reason.

I focussed on the door, making it fling open while using my energy to knock Tim out of the way at the same time.

Both of them looked shocked. Tim looked around from where he lay at the bottom of the stairs. Emma looked at Tim, then at the open door.

"RUN!" I bellowed.

Emma jumped back as if she heard me, then dashed out of the house. I stayed behind to guard Tim until I could no longer hear her feet pounding down the street.

Tim got up and counted out his money. Although, I noticed his hands shaking. It added up to £2,500. I was worth even less than I first thought. I told myself that wasn't important. He had the I.D. I could move things, but I never learned how to pick up objects for long enough to take them from one place to another when there were miles between the two places. If I wanted to get the potential evidence back from him, I would need to get help before the police searched my bedroom at my mum's house.

I left Tim to his money, received for doing something he clearly enjoyed doing. I had more important things to do, like make sure he got arrested before he got the opportunity to kill again.

I thought about Steve, knowing it was a risk because I was using up a lot of energy again. It was a bad idea so soon after making the door open and throwing Tim backwards, away from my sister. I went ahead and transported myself anyway.

I made sure I appeared outside Steve's door, recalling that he didn't like to be caught off guard, and it had to be around five in the morning.

It took me more than a few attempts to make the doorbell ring, but I wanted to make Steve's first impression of me as a ghost a good one.

After I waited a few minutes, Steve opened the door.

"You, from the other day," he said.

"I'm dead now, but that's not important. I've dealt with it, but I do need your help, please."

"What?" he asked, rubbing his eyes, maybe hoping I would vanish so that he could go back to bed.

"I need your help to catch a killer, but the good news is, I know who he is and who hired him. However, I'm dead, which means getting that information to the police will be problematic. That's why I need your help. Nobody else can see me."

Chapter Eighteen

It took a while, but I explained to Steve what happened. I told him about my first death, then becoming a ghost – before I was alive again – as temporarily as it was.

"So, we've met before? Other than when you knocked on my door sounding like a crazy person?"

"Exactly, and you tried to help me get proof of my killer. It didn't work out and I got you in trouble, but I have proof of who killed me now, or at least I will if you help me."

He scratched the back of his head, I looked around at the downstairs of his house. It was still well lived in and crying out for a good clean.

"What if me helping you gets me in trouble? Maybe that's a fixed event."

"It's not. You responded to my sister's request for a ghost-writer last time. And you were hanging around the restaurant where I used to work. Emma and Tim used all that against you. If you stay away from the restaurant and my sister this time, they won't even find out about you helping me."

He looked around at his bookcases. "I'm not sure. How did you get me to help you last time?"

"I showed up at random times without knocking or saying boo and I annoyed you into helping me. I can do that again if you really want me to. I'm trying to be nicer and less irritating this time. Plus, the whole haunting you thing was hard work, but you're the only one who can help me. More women will die. I could have tried to avoid my own death, but I was counting on my murder leading to Tim's arrest."

He stared at me before saying, "okay. What can I do?"

"Great, I thought you'd never ask. So, while I was bleeding to death, I used my blood to write his name on a nearby bin. Before that, I left the I.D Shelly and I stole. Like I said though, Emma took it and gave it back to him when she paid him for a job well done. I need to get it back and the police need to know about the bin, if they don't already."

I felt sure that the police would be professional enough to have spotted the name in blood right next to my dead body, but I had to be certain.

"When you say you need to get the I.D back, you mean you need me to get it back for you?" he asked.

"I'm a ghost," I reminded him. "I can move things sometimes, but not a driving license all the way to the police station miles away, even if I knew how to make the police understand what it is, if I just float it to them. Besides, even if I could do all of that it would use up more energy than it would take to make me blink out of existence for a while. Someone else could die by then. They did last time."

"No pressure then," he said, but at least that meant he would do it.

"We need a plan," I told him, not wanting a repeat of when he had almost been caught by Paul, back when I suspected he was my killer. Even though I did enjoy the part where I made the shovel attack Paul. I allowed myself to smirk for a moment as I recalled that night.

I knew Tim would be looking for his next victim. I also knew who the second victim would be. So, I suggested helping Steve to break into Tim's house while he went out, probably searching for victim number two. I could open the locks to let Steve in, although I wasn't sure how long it would take me. Hopefully, I wouldn't black out as a side-effect. I must have almost reached my quota of energy, I told myself.

"If I disappear for a little while, you need to get out of there. I won't be able to help you if he comes home and finds you there," I warned.

"This is weird for me. You talk like we're friends, as if you're worried about me. I don't remember you, except for the mad rant on my doorstep."

"You're the only one who helped me," I said.

"It sounds like you didn't have too many choices," he retorted, looking uncomfortable at the idea of a ghost woman caring about him. "Besides, if I'm the only one who helped you, why did you repay me by knocking on my door and insulting me?"

"It wasn't supposed be an insult. I was trying to help, but I didn't have much time. I don't think I helped people much before. This is all new for me."

I knew it was strange, but I considered him a friend from my first time as a ghost.

I gave him the second victims name to search for information about; such as her address, workplace or even where she liked to hang out with friends. While he busied himself with that, I returned to Tim's house to keep watch so I could let Steve know the moment he left the house.

If I hadn't thought of my murderer as a sick creep before, what I saw over the next few days was more than enough to convince me.

The morning papers were delivered. Even though my injuries weren't pictured, they were described in graphic detail. A smiling picture of me sat above the headline, "local woman brutally murdered in city centre." Is there a non-brutal way of being murdered? Maybe death by poisoned chocolate cake would be considered nicer, but the end result would be the same. Given the choice, I would opt for the cake though.

Tim lay in bed with the article beside him. Let's just say he recited the whole thing three times, getting more and more excitable with each recital until he made the newspaper unreadable. I knew that killing me had awakened something inside him: something that had been there unacted on for many years. I saw it the night Emma gave him his I.D back and paid him. He would have done the job for free. Emma wasn't to know that though. It was only while I watched him, before turning away with disgust, I realised just how vile he was. I couldn't get my head round how much sexual pleasure he gained from remembering what he had done to me.

After two days, he dressed and left the house. I appeared back at Steve's to tell him the house was empty. Twenty minutes later, Steve arrived in a taxi. He waited until it pulled away before talking to me.

"How long will he be gone?" His eyes darted around, reminding me of the stickers I used to get at the dentist, usually an animal of some sort with wobbly eyes. I wasn't sure if he felt nervous about Tim returning, or the chance of someone noticing him standing in the street talking to himself.

"I'm a ghost, not a psychic," I pointed out, then passed through the locked door.

It took me a few attempts to unlock it for Steve, but I managed.

"Did you bring gloves?" I asked.

"Do I really need these?" he complained, putting on a pair of disposable gloves – like the ones you get when you buy a box of hair dye.

"The last thing we need is for you to get your fingerprints on anything," I told him. "Don't you watch crime thrillers?"

"I prefer comedies. My life is more of a rom-com, without the rom…or the com." Steve replied. He walked through me in his haste to get the breaking and entering over with. "Where do you want me to start?"

It occurred to me that Tim might have taken his driving license with him in his wallet. Although, it's possible he was wary of anyone getting hold of it after losing it once already. His use of false names proved he didn't want anyone to know his true identity. He may have planned to do something long before he killed me, even if it wasn't murder.

"Well?" Steve persisted.

"Ssh, I'm trying to think like a sick creep with a fetish for hurting women."

"And, how's that going?"

"Well, obviously I'm not a sick creep, so it's a work-in-progress." I paused before saying, "If I was him, I wouldn't take anything with me that could identify me to potential victims. I wouldn't throw everything away though. People always need I.D for all kinds of reasons. Instead, I would hide it."

"That's all very interesting Inspector Casper, but where would you hide it?"

I ignored his new sarcastic name for me. People probably called me worse things when I was alive, despite me never realising it at the time.

I walked up the stairs. Steve followed until we reached Tim's bedroom. He stopped to stare at the newspaper on Tim's bed. The image of me smiling (obviously during happier times) was unrecognisable because of the mess Tim had made.

"What's that?" Steve asked, reaching down to pick up the paper.

I assumed he meant the stains obscuring most of the article.

"You don't want to touch that," I warned.

Steve looked at me as if waiting for an explanation, before screwing up his face.

"Eugh!" He pulled his hand back and leapt away as if it might launch itself off the newspaper and physically attack him. That in itself would be a front-page news story.

I went to the chest of drawers. "I'm thinking, maybe in one of these or under the mattress," I suggested.

Steve lifted the mattress while I peered underneath.

"Anything?" he asked.

I knelt to look. "No, try the drawers."

He did, starting from the bottom. There were plenty of magazines and books, mostly true crime.

"Why doesn't that surprise me? To him, those are probably wank mags," Steve said.

He searched the other drawers, only finding clothes until just the top one remained to search.

"I'm not going through his underwear," Steve complained, after opening the drawer to reveal numerous pairs of socks and underpants. "I've seen what he did to that newspaper article."

"I need the I.D," I reminded him.

"It might not be in there."

"But it might, and you're wearing gloves," I pointed out.

He rooted through the drawer, sighing and muttering to make his reluctance clear. He threw items out, wearing a pained expression across his face when I asked him to put them back. I didn't want Tim figuring out someone had been in his house and gone through his things.

"Is this it?" he asked, pulling out the driving license between his thumb and forefinger as if it might bite his hand off.

"That's it," I yelped, making him jump backwards and almost fall onto the bed, while twisting his head and looking at it as though it was a pool of lava he mustn't fall into.

"For someone who sees dead people, you scare easy," I said.

"Let's get out of here."

His nervous expression reminded me that Tim could return at any time.

"I'll meet you back at your house," I told him.

Steve shoved the I.D into the back pocket of his jeans and fled the room. I heard his feet pounding down the stairs.

The next part of my plan was trickier. My mum left the house less often than Steve did, preferring to sit in her favourite chair watching soaps and sobbing at random intervals. It wasn't that I didn't want her to care I was gone, but it no longer seemed as important as getting the evidence back to where I left it the first time around.

I stayed at my mum's, watching as she cried, eating only small amounts of food before throwing close to whole platefuls away. I tried to decide if getting Steve to return the I.D to my old bedroom was the best option. Or should I find somewhere new to put it, where the police would find it and Emma wouldn't?

The phone rang. Mum answered with "hello" in her posh phone voice.

Someone spoke, but I didn't hear what they said.

"Yes, I'm in all day today, but I don't know what you think you'll find. She wasn't killed here," she said, bursting into tears again as she spoke the k word.

There was a pause as she sniffed down the phone, then a male voice said something else which I couldn't understand from where I stood at the bottom of the stairs.

"Yes, if it's procedure. Whatever helps to catch this maniac." She hung up.

"No," I said. The police couldn't be searching my mum's house for evidence yet. The driving licence wasn't in my room. They wouldn't find anything to link

Tim to my murder. I had an idea, but I doubted it would work. With no other options presenting themselves, I gave it a try.

I transported myself to Steve's house, feeling a little guilty about interrupting while he sat at his laptop writing an article. I spotted a sentence about endangered species.

"You like animals?" I asked, forgetting the way he preferred me to knock, or at least do something less intimidating than appearing behind him and talking without warning.

"Shit," he yelled, almost falling off his chair. He looked up at me, his eyes locked on mine, as he said, "Yes, they don't barge into my house and scare the shit out of me. That's why I prefer them to you."

"Sorry, I don't have much time. Do you have the evidence we took from Tim's house?"

He stood up and opened the desk drawer as he asked, "is your mum out?"

I saw the licence in the open desk drawer, inside a see-through sandwich bag. I raised my eyebrows at him.

"I didn't have one of those evidence bags they use on TV."

"I thought you didn't watch crime thrillers."

"I don't."

I shook my head, remembering the urgency of what I needed to do. "My mum is home, but the police are going there today. So, I'm going to try something."

"What?"

"To take it there myself."

Steve gawked at me. I couldn't blame him. Even if I managed it, the chances were high that it would exert my ghost energy and I'd have a blackout.

"You'll keep an eye on the investigation in whatever way you can, if I don't get back from my enforced ghost nap in time to save the next victim?" I asked.

He nodded, his expression a mixture of concern and fear. "I'll do what I can," he promised.

Chapter Nineteen

Holding the driving licence while transporting myself, proved to be a challenge. It took nine attempts before I arrived back at my mum's house with it still in my hand. I kept dropping it at the moment I was about to leave Steve's house. I had no idea how much time I had before the police would show up. I headed towards my bedroom straightaway but dropped the licence on the stairs. No amount of swiping my hand towards it would work. My fingers kept passing through it and the stairs. Something as simple as picking up a small object required more concentration than when I wrote my dissertation. My mind raced with thoughts of the police officers who could be arriving at any moment, to search the house for clues about my final hours and who might have killed me, making it hard for me to focus on anything else.

The thumping at the door interrupted my final attempt. I staggered backwards, only managing to compose myself in time to stop when I reached the bottom. I was grateful that I hadn't lost control to the extent where I fell through the floor. That was always disconcerting.

My mum hurried to the door and let two policemen into the house.

"Mrs Winters," one of them said. His eyes rested on her for a moment before wandering to the hallway. I assumed he was keen to get the search over with. "As my colleague explained on the phone, this is just procedure. We wouldn't be doing our job if we didn't search the victims last known address."

"Sarah," my mum said. "My daughter's name is Sarah, not victim."

"Of course," the other man spoke up. "Shall we get started?"

His colleague nodded before walking down the hallway. He checked the drawers and shone a small torch into the space underneath the stairs. I stood as the second police officer passed by me. I followed him up the steps. It seemed like I should, since my mum was pre-occupied with following the one downstairs.

"Look down," I instructed.

As usual I was ignored, but he was going to pass the step where the I.D had fallen. His eyes focussed on the way ahead, rather than looking down for the evidence below where his feet were about to tread. I could tell he wasn't as meticulous as his colleague.

There were no familiar signs of dizziness, so I decided to risk what I did next.

I stood beside him and yelled into his ear, "look down now."

He gazed at the spot where I stood — his eyes a little wider than normal, but like most people he stared through me. To his credit, he looked down though.

The I.D (featuring Tim with his psychotic stare) caught his eye. He crouched to pick it up. I knelt from a few steps above him and watched. His eyes fell to the name. I saw something there, maybe a glint of recognition. It made sense if the police had seen the bin with the same name written in my blood, which I assume would have been tested to confirm it was mine.

He took it to his friend downstairs. My mum was in the kitchen making tea by that point. The officers talked to each other in hushed voices.

"Could be, although that looked more like Tom."

I grasped that in the dark I was unable to see, and my writing could have looked like it spelt out the name Tom, or maybe the blood dripped. I was dying and so unable to produce nice neat letters. I figured I should be grateful I wasn't murdered by someone with a much longer name.

"What's going on?" Mum interrupted from the doorway of the front room, clutching a mug of tea in each hand. She entered the room and placed them down on the coffee table when neither officer responded.

The shorter of the two cleared his throated and took the licence from his partner. "Have you seen this before?"

"No," she shook her head, "And I've never seen him before either, nor would I want to." She pulled a face and shivered.

I was pleased to witness how the image of Tim had the same effect on her as it did on me. I accept that most killers are someone's friend or family and they can look normal, attractive even, but Tim's face screamed a warning to run for the hills. The problem is, he was the sort of person who would pursue you up those hills, kill you and get off on the whole experience before burying your body up there.

"Did he kill my daughter? I thought Paul…"

"We don't know, but we would like to speak to him," the other officer said.

My mum stared at him, her eyes conveying more stubbornness than anything she could possibly have said. She wasn't about to let them leave without an explanation.

"He's a person of interest," is all the officer said.

Mum's expression softened a little, despite him only saying the same thing in a different way. I could tell he wouldn't disclose any more details just yet. I decided to tell Steve what happened, so he wouldn't be getting stressed about the possibility of having to investigate my killer alone, or carry the weight of Tim's future victims on his conscience.

I transported myself back to his house.

"Knock knock," my voice was low as I tried to stay at least five-feet away, so as not to startle him again.

I recapped what happened.

"It's good that the police got the I.D after all of that, and that they saw the name on the bin too, even if they mistook it for Tom. They're the police, they'll figure it out."

"But?" I asked, seeing that his expression conveyed how he thought it was anything but great.

"You've used up a lot of energy in a short space of time."

"I've been thinking the same thing, I should have blacked out by now," I admitted.

"Maybe…" he began.

There was no way I could drop the subject when he seemed like he might have an idea about why I was still there, rather than taking an enforced ghost nap.

He seemed to realise this and elaborated. "It might be something to do with the voice of God?"

"Huh?"

"The voice you hear; it's God, right? The one who sent you back and said this was all an interview."

"I can't remember if he said test or interview. It happened so fast, and I'm not sure he's God. He's...a higher power of some kind," I relented. "You think he gave me unlimited energy, like unlimited lives in a computer game?"

"Something like that, unless you've got any better ideas. Maybe it's part of the test or interview, to see how far you would go when you think you're at risk of blacking out."

"Oh," I said, as I processed his theory. "Is there anything about this in your books?"

"Nothing I've come across, and I've read them all more than a few times."

I looked around the room at the bookcases. My mind made a quick estimate that there must be around two hundred books.

"Right, we need to get you out of here, you've been a recluse way too long," I announced,

"I'm not a recluse, I went out just last week to research a chain of shops that are closing down, for a freelance article I'm writing. On the way back, I popped into the supermarket and stocked up on food."

"Wow," I feigned surprise. "You're really living a wild life."

He looked at me, his eyebrows raised as if trying to suggest I wasn't living a wild life either.

"I'm dead. What's your excuse?" I asked.

He shrugged.

I saw my chance to repay Steve for his help. At the last minute, I had knocked on Steve's door to try to get him to change his life, but it ended up sounding like a rant. It turns out, you can't just turn up on someone's doorstep and give what you wrongly consider to be a motivational speech when they don't know who you are, then expect them to be changed for the better. Now with my potentially endless ghost energy, I could get him out of the house and be his invisible wing-woman.

"What are you planning?" he asked, his arms crossed against his chest.

"First of all, that is some closed off body language right there," I pointed out. "You can't be doing that when you're talking to a woman in a bar."

"I'm going to be talking to a woman in a bar?"

"Damn right you're going to be talking to a woman in a bar," I confirmed.

Despite Steve's protest, the two of us ended up in a bar in the Northern Quarter. It seemed nice enough. The little booths gave the place a cosy feel, but I didn't let Steve get comfortable. I made him sit on one of the stools at the bar, by repeating for him to sit there over and over. He relented, if only to shut me up.

I watched the door while he ordered himself a pint. A woman entered — pretty and blonde, in her early thirties. I was about to turn to Steve and suggest he strike up a conversation with her when a man walked in behind her. He was blonde too, taller than her by at least a foot. His arms were twice the size of Steve's, in a gym workout way; not a too much time spent eating doughnuts way.

He leant down as she turned around. Their arms wrapped around each other, his around her shoulders, hers around his waist. Neither seemed bothered about blocking the door as their faces inched closer until their mouths met. I could tell they considered themselves to be the hottest couple in town and they wanted everyone in the bar to know it. The door opened and the boyfriend acted as a buffer. It hit his back, but he didn't move. He twisted his head away, then let go of the woman and turned to face the brunette as she tried to squeeze through the gap. The blonde glared at the woman as though she and her demi-god of a boyfriend had every right to block the entrance if they were making out.

"Sorry." The brunette didn't sound like she regretted anything, other than not pushing the door harder and knocking the pair of them over.

Steve watched as the woman sat down on the next stool but one.

"Say something to her," I hissed at Steve.

He looked at me. His eyes seemed to be pleading with me, either to go away or tell him what he should say.

"Just copy me." I said. "I would have slammed the door into the pair of them."

She was ordering a vodka and coke by then. Steve kept his mouth shut. So, I repeated myself. He must have known how this would play out by that point — with me acting like a broken record until he copied what I said. I wasn't being cruel. It was the only way I could think of to get him to meet new people. I wasn't an expert myself, despite what I believed when I was alive.

"I would have slammed the door into the pair of them," Steve said.

"Now laugh, just a small laugh, don't overdo it," I instructed, as the woman turned to face him.

He didn't laugh, though he managed a half-smile. It would have to do.

"Sometimes I think love makes people selfish," she responded with a smile of her own.

She wasn't obviously pretty like the blonde, but she had a likable face. I could imagine she was popular when she was at school, probably at work too.

"Oh yeah?" Steve asked.

"Look at it this way, you get so absorbed with another person. Before you know it, you're blocking doorways and not caring about whether anyone else wants a drink at the end of a very long day."

"Ask her why her day was long," I urged.

I could see his eyes sneaking a glance at me, before darting back to her.

"Bad day?" he asked.

"The worst, but you don't want to hear about that."

"I'm not doing anything else," I whispered into Steve's ear. He duly repeated my words, sounding more convincing than I expected.

She opened her mouth to answer, but I stopped listening. The door opened. The couple were seated, so avoided getting knocked into again. The man who entered the bar was Tim. He looked around as if searching for someone. His eyes cast over Steve's potential new friend. Lust flashed in the killer's eyes before he went to a booth by himself.

Chapter Twenty

I was still deciding what to do, when my sister walked into the bar. Her hair was bleached blonde, but as distant as we used to be, I still recognised her. She looked around in much the same way Tim had. She walked in between the booths until her eyes fell on him.

I left Steve to talk to the woman on his own, as I wandered over to get a closer look at what was going on between my sister and my murderer now. Did he want to extort more money from her? Or maybe she found someone else for him to kill.

He looked up at her before pointing to the seat next to him. Emma sat, a bit like the Labrador the neighbours adopted when we were kids. Her blonde hair reminded me of that same Labrador, Dory. I shook my head. It wasn't the time to be thinking about the neighbours' dog. She had more humanity than my sister did anyway. Dory followed me to school every day, then waited outside at the end of the day to walk me home. I never understood how she knew what time it was. My point is, not once did the dog pay some sicko to kill me, so that's why I preferred her to my sister.

"What did you do?" Tim hissed at Emma. His fingers clamped around her arm.

She squirmed as she said, "I didn't do anything. I got the I.D back for you, remember? You're the one who let that slut steal if from you in the first place."

"Then you called me out of the blue and say the police have it. How do you suppose that happened?"

"I don't know." The way she shook her head reminded me of an alternative version of the nodding dog from the adverts. Again with the dogs. I'm not sure why I kept thinking about them. Maybe it was because of the way my sister acted – like an animal, only worse. Animal behaviour comes down to survival. I was never a threat to Emma. She would have survived just fine without having me killed.

"Are you double-crossing me?" Tim accused.

"No, I swear." She pulled her arm from his grasp and got to her feet.

"You should remember, if I get arrested for this, I tell the police everything."

"I'll fix it," Emma promised.

Emma turned to leave, and I took a step to follow her. I glanced over at Steve. He was deep in conversation with the brunette. I felt bad leaving him there after I dragged him out of his comfort zone. This was my sister hinting that she would obstruct the investigation into my murder though. Her attempts to save her own skin would get more women killed — innocent women who hadn't paid someone to kill their own sisters. The decision was made. I wanted to follow Emma, but another glance at Tim with his eyes transfixed on the woman talking to Steve, told me Steve's new friend might be in trouble. Tim smiled and walked over, despite Steve sitting right there. I watched Emma leave, the door swung shut behind her. I had to stay. He may have found a new victim, one he hadn't spotted before and it was all my fault. My actions had led to this change of events.

"I'm sorry to interrupt, I'm Neil," Tim lied.

Steve recognised him. I could tell by the way his gaze fell to me, like he was waiting for me to instruct him on what to do.

"Don't let him leave here with her," I warned.

"I'm Julia and this is Steve," she said. "But I'm afraid I'm not interested. I'm talking to Steve."

I fought the urge to swear. Now Steve was on Tim's radar again. I didn't want that to happen, not after the last time.

"I'll tell you what," Tim said, his voice slurred as if suddenly drunk. He was sober only minutes earlier while threatening Emma. "Me, you and a game of pool," he challenged Steve.

"For what?" Steve looked at Tim, then at Julia before his eyes fell on me.

"The woman," Tim announced.

"Tell him not to be ridiculous," I said.

"Don't be ridiculous. She's a person, not a prize to be won in a game of pool."

Julia gave Steve a grateful smile. She turned to Tim.

"How about a counter offer? If Steve beats you at pool, you leave us alone?"

"And if I win?"

Julia reached for her purse and looked inside. "I'll give you £30."

She didn't know her £30 was nothing, compared to the £2,500 Emma paid him.

"Alright," he agreed, but I suspected he had something else up his sleeve.

I made sure Steve won. With every ball that dangled over the pocket, I gave it a small amount of encouragement to drop. Each shot when Steve was a little off, I managed to divert the ball back on track with a seventy-five percent success rate. It was a little more difficult, but a hundred percent success rate would have caused suspicion anyway,

"No way," Tim snapped, his bottom lip trembled as if he might cry.

I began to add information to my psychological profile of Tim. It struck me that he was used to getting what he wanted one way or another. I guessed his parents spoiled him as a child, thinking they were doing the right thing. I would have been surprised to learn he had siblings, but maybe he did and they no longer stayed in touch with him. He could be the black sheep of the family. Maybe that played a part in why he became a killer — after discovering life wouldn't work out the way it was while growing up and getting everything he wanted, then his family cut him out of their lives because he became too demanding. It seemed plausible. Although, not every disillusioned person becomes a killer. So, he obviously had underlying psychological problems to begin with, whatever his background story happened to be.

"Time for you to get home, I think," Julia suggested.

Steve glared at Tim. If I didn't know him, I would find the look somewhat threatening.

Tim grunted, muttering something under his breath as he left. Like a miracle had occurred, he became sober again. His steps towards the door were in a straight line, where previously they resembled those of someone who spun around in circles before attempting to walk.

"He's not going to give up that easily," I guessed.

"Maybe I should walk you home, in case he hangs around outside," Steve said.

"He did look like the kind of person who hangs out in dark alleys, but I'll be fine." She didn't grasp how close to the truth her words were.

Steve looked at me for guidance again.

"Give her your number to call you when she gets home."

He wrote his number on a blank space at the bottom of a beer mat, then handed it to her.

"Let me know when you get home, so I don't worry. This isn't a pick-up line, but I really didn't get a good vibe from that guy. After you call me, you can bin this if you like."

"Thank you." She took the beer mat, dropping it into her bag. "I might keep the number. It's not every day someone plays and wins a game of pool for my honour." She flashed him a smile which seemed to brighten up her face. Maybe I would even have found her attractive if I was a man…and alive.

Steve watched her all the way to the door with an expression I hadn't seen on his face before. I could tell that he liked her. He was concerned about Tim getting to her. I don't know why this surprised me. Steve was a loner, only venturing out of his house when he had to. I forced him out to a bar to prepare him for meeting and connecting with someone else, someone living. I never thought about him meeting that someone else so soon though.

"It's okay, I've got this," I said, not waiting for a response before I went after her. I passed through the door and out into the street. She stood on the corner where the taxis usually park up to wait for customers, but there wasn't a taxi in sight. People spilled out of nearby pubs, bars and restaurants as others shoved their way in, as if to take their places. It was a busy night for taxi drivers.

Julia looked from left to right, then crossed the road, presumably towards the nearest bus stop. She didn't make it though. I spotted Tim racing after her, before she heard his footsteps over the nearby traffic. I thought he couldn't try anything without someone in one of the passing cars spotting him and intervening. He proved me wrong by grabbing her arms.

"What are you doing?" Julia yelled. She pulled away, one foot backing into the road. The driver of a blue car beeped the horn and swerved to avoid her. The car failed to stop though.

"What are you doing?" I shouted too, but at the car which was in the distance by then. "She needs help."

"You owe me a conversation," Tim said, retrieving one of her arms and tugging her back onto the pavement. He kept a tight grip on her.

"My friend beat you at pool, that was the deal."

"How about we change the deal to you becoming a decent person and being civil to me. I haven't done anything to you. Just talk to me"

"Okay, what would you like to talk about?"

Tim let go of Julia's arm and smiled. "That's better." He walked towards the alley between two shops. "Let's talk."

"Down there? Why can't we talk here?" she asked.

"Privacy."

"I've got to get home," Julia turned and began to walk away, taking long strides.

"Get back here, bitch," Tim snapped, reminding me of someone possessed by a demon in a horror movie. His mouth contorted into a grimace. He caught up with Julia and slammed her into a wall.

She gasped and tried to speak. Cars continued to pass, but not one of the drivers stopped to offer any assistance.

"Help," she managed to squeak.

"Do you want to talk now?" he asked, trying to drag her away to somewhere more secluded I guessed. "You want me to help you?"

I closed my eyes, hoping that the theory Steve and I came up with about me having unlimited energy was right. I concentrated on materialising the way I did at Tim's house. I was afraid for my sister then. Anger fuelled me this time, anger that Tim was about to take another life — the life of the first woman (possibly in years) who had showed an interest in Steve.

"No, she wants my help," I said, becoming corporeal in front of him.

He let go of Julia and staggered backwards. "You?"

"Oh, how sweet. You remember me. Well, I guess you never forget your first time; not to mentioned how long you must have spent wanking over that article of me. My face probably appears in your wet dreams all the time now." I walked forwards as he crawled backwards. "Let's see if we can change those dreams into waking nightmares."

Julia looked at me, then at the road. I thought she might run, which would have been the best thing for her to do, but it seemed a little rude when as far as she knew, I had stopped to help her. She couldn't realise I was a ghost.

I shoved Tim into the wall to see how he liked it, which wasn't that much, judging by the pained expression on his face.

Julia ran, but only towards the road. She called for help as cars tried to swerve around her. Tim regained enough composure to run in the opposite direction to the car pulling up to find out what was going on.

"He tried to attack me," Julia said.

"Who? Him?" the man asked as he climbed out of the vehicle. He was tall and would have towered over Tim, likely causing him to soil himself. That idea made me smile to myself. He had humiliated me by grinding against me as I bled out. He gained sexual pleasure from the act of me dying. Smiling at him soiling himself, felt like some kind of karma even if only in my imagination.

"Yes," Julia said, as the passenger side of the car opened.

"Are you okay?" a woman asked. She didn't look okay herself. Her hands were on her expansive stomach. She was barely held up by a pair of skinny legs as her drawn out words gave away the exertion from just standing there. It seemed obvious she was pregnant. I asked myself if I could deliver a baby. I doubted I could while alive, so why would I be able to while dead?

Tim rounded the corner at the end of the road, disappearing out of sight.

"Get back in the car, love," the man told his wife.

"Not until I know she's okay."

"He's gone now. I'm really sorry, but my wife and I are on the way to the hospital. She's having a baby," he explained.

Julia looked in my direction, but I was no longer visible. "There was a woman, she helped me, I think."

"Okay, well, the guy who tried to attack you is gone now. Maybe she scared him off," he suggested.

"We should at least give her a lift to the police station on our way to the hospital," the woman suggested, clutching the car door as a contraction started.

"No, go. I'll make my own way there," Julia said. Her skin was drained of colour. I wasn't sure if it was because of Tim, or the possibility of the woman and her husband driving her to the police station and the woman giving birth on the way.

They both got back into the car, leaving Julia standing on the kerb. I followed her to the police station, not wanting to risk Tim trying again if he decided to lurk somewhere nearby, rather than return home unsatisfied.

Chapter Twenty-One

"Hey." I tried not to shout as I appeared in Steve's front room.

"Is she alright?"

I realised he had been waiting to hear if Julia made it home okay. So, I wasted no time in relaying what had happened after Julia left the bar.

"Were we right? You're not going to have any ghost blackouts?" Steve asked after I reassured him that Julia wasn't in any immediate danger. "You would have blacked out by now."

"It seems that way," I said.

"Do you think the police will be able to arrest Tim from Julia's statement?" he asked.

"I'm not sure; it was dark and they might ask her how she recognised him."

"But I could be a witness, I'll say I saw him harassing her in the bar."

"Maybe," I said, "but I should get back to the police station to make sure she's okay."

Steve smiled gratefully. I felt a pang of jealousy. I recalled my earlier thoughts that I could have fallen for someone like Steve. He wasn't mine though, he couldn't be. I was dead; he was alive. That was a major barrier to any potential relationship we might have. He needed to get out of his house and live his life. He needed someone like Julia for that, not a dead woman intent on catching a killer. He couldn't take me home to meet his parents.

I arrived back at the station. Julia sat in the waiting area.

"Miss Lorrenson?" a woman asked, standing over her. She seemed a little young, possibly in her early twenties, and lanky. I didn't fancy her chances against someone like Tim if she was the arresting officer. He might push her once and send her toppling over.

"Yes," Julia looked up, her face dropped as if she might be thinking along the same lines as me.

"I'm Sophie. You say someone attacked you?"

"Yes. I mean he tried, but a woman came along and helped me, then a couple stopped their car to check I was okay. If they hadn't..." her voice trailed off.

"Come with me. I'll take your statement," her voice lowered, as if she had lost interest and had hoped for something juicier than an almost attack.

"He's a murderer, he would have killed her," I spoke up, but I was firmly stuck in ghost mode again. Making myself visible would cause endless confusion. I had no way to explain who I was without coming off like a crazy person. My body lay cold in the morgue or buried somewhere. I didn't even know if I managed to miss my own funeral. I tried to focus and not become distracted by imagining who turned up and what they said.

In the interview room, Julia began to explain the events of the night, starting with the bar.

"I got talking to a guy in a bar," she said.

"This is the guy who tried to attack you?" Sophie asked.

"No, this guy, Steve was nice; a little shy and nervous. Not cocky like the guy who tried to cut him off. He sent off major creep vibes. You know the sort, when you just know. You're a police officer, you must get those instincts more than most."

"Sometimes," Sophie admitted. "So, this second guy. What was his name?"

"Neil, I think that's what he said."

"Shit," I swore. How were the police meant to do their job and catch this guy when he kept using fake names, so they couldn't put the pieces together and question whether he was the same guy who killed me?

"It might not be his real name though," Julia suggested. "Creeps like that don't always use their real names. At university, the same guy chatted me up three weeks in a row. He used a different name each time, but I remembered him. He obviously didn't remember me though, he put it about so much."

"Can we get back to what happened tonight with Neil?" Sophie looked bored.

"Yes, sorry. I was making a point though."

"What was it about Neil that gave you bad vibes?"

"Creepy vibes. He was persistent. Most men will take no for an answer. He wouldn't, even after I told him I was there with Steve, but he wanted to play pool for me like I was a trophy, then even after he lost the game, he hung around outside and grabbed my arm as I tried to walk to the bus stop."

"So, he grabbed your arm?" Sophie asked, writing in her notebook.

"It was more than that. He said I owed him, or something like that and he tried to drag me away from the main road to somewhere quieter."

"He didn't actually drag you anywhere?"

"No, because that woman showed up and the car pulled up afterwards."

"Witnesses, okay." Sophie looked relieved and a little more interested. "Can you describe the woman and the occupants of the car?"

"The woman was a redhead, about my height, but super strong. The way she shoved that creep against the wall, then got him down on the ground. I'm not sure whether she pushed him again or he fell, but he looked terrified of her."

"And the person or people in the car?"

"A tall guy, dark hair. The woman was blonde. They were on the way to the hospital because her waters broke. The car was blue, but I can't remember the make."

"Okay, I should be able to track them down by contacting the local hospitals. What about the guy who almost attacked you?" Her question sounded like more of an afterthought.

"Dark hair, short for a guy, not fat, but not skinny either. He had a chubby face though, and brown eyes that stare straight through you in a creepy mentally undressing you way."

"Anything else?" Sophie made notes.

"He needs to be caught before he hurts someone, if he hasn't already."

"What makes you assume that? More vibes?"

"Something like that," Julia answered.

"I don't suppose you have a number for Steve?"

"I do, but he can't tell you more than I already have. I left the bar alone. He wasn't there when Neil caught up with me."

"Write it down anyway." Sophie tore a piece of paper from her pad and pushed it towards Julia, along with a pen.

Sophie also asked for Julia's contact details. Then she walked to the door, opening it as a signal for Julia to leave.

"What happens now?" Julia asked.

"We'll talk to the witnesses, but even if we find this guy, it's a caution at best. We can't take someone to court for vibes or grabbing you by your arm. If anything, he might decide to press charges against this woman. It sounds like she hurt him a lot more than he hurt your arm."

"In that case, I hope you never find her," Julia snapped, then stormed out of the room.

I followed her. It was early morning when she left the station, a few hours from sunrise. I told myself I would let Steve know she was okay after I saw her home safely.

She took out her phone and a number from a scrap of paper in her hand.

"Steve?" she asked, moments later.

"Yes, it's me. I'm okay. You sound concerned."

Silence, as Steve talked on the other end of the phone. I considered using my bonus energy to put the call on hands-free to enable me to hear what he was saying. I assumed that couldn't be part of any test I was given by the godlike presence from the darkness though.

"Give me your address. I'll come over, I need to talk to you, but it's going to sound a little out there."

She hung up and looked in my direction, staring through me as most people did, I guessed.

"Who are you?"

Could she see me? I didn't know what to say. She spoke again before I had time to come up with something.

"I know you're there, even though I can't see you. And I'm guessing you saved me last night. So, thank you for that." She turned and flagged down a passing taxi, giving the driver Steve's address.

When she arrived, I went inside while she rang the doorbell.

"Things are about to get interesting," I warned Steve as he answered the door.

I wasn't wrong.

"Are you okay?" Steve asked, forgetting he wasn't meant to know as much as he did about what happened.

"Yes, are you? You know somehow, don't you?"

Steve looked at me, but it wasn't for me to try to explain.

"I've always been sensitive, sensing things that other people either don't notice or they pass them off as Deja Vu, a shiver or some other explanation."

"Okay," Steve said. He was facing her, but his right eye moved to glance at me.

"Don't get me wrong. I don't claim to see ghosts, but something happened to me. I think somehow you know about it. Did you sense the same thing I did? Is that how you knew? You seemed concerned, like you sensed what that guy is capable of too," she insisted.

"It's okay. She'll believe you," I encouraged.

"I see ghosts," Steve said.

Julia managed a small smile. "Yeah, right."

He looked at me pointedly. I shrugged.

"Shit, you're not kidding. Is she here? The woman who saved me from that pervert. She's here, isn't she? And she's a ghost?" She glanced around the room as if expecting me to materialise. Her eyes screwing up slightly at Steve's living conditions. "It smells in here. Is that what dead people smell like?"

"Don't you dare blame me for your lousy housekeeping," I snapped.

"No, that's my bad housekeeping," he admitted. He blushed, failing to meet Julia's eyes.

I found it easy to relate as her eyes kept drifting around the room — even though she must have wanted to learn more about Steve's gift. The state of Steve's living conditions had that effect on me too, even though it became tolerable over time.

"You can really see ghosts?" she asked.

I waited as patiently as I could while Steve told her everything I already knew, including how we met.

"Not on the doorstep," I corrected.

He looked at me, prompting Julia to guess I was talking to him.

"What's she saying?"

"She's reminding me I met her before she showed up on my doorstep telling me to sort my life out. I don't remember that though," he insisted.

Julia remained silent while he told her about the first time I died, then continued with his story.

"That's amazing," she said, when he was done.

"Amazing as in I should be committed to a specialist hospital?"

'No, just amazing. I've always felt like there was something else. But how many times do you get first-hand experience of a ghost? A ghost saved my life tonight. And you…you see them and talk to them all the time."

"I try to avoid talking to them or even letting them though I can see them, present company excluded," he added, looking in my direction.

"Why would you do that? I would have questions, so many questions." Her enthusiasm was overwhelming; as if she had just found proof that Santa Claus, The Tooth Fairy, elves and unicorns were all real.

When the excitement died down and Julia began to grasp Steve's reason for not been as elated about his gift as she was, she wanted to know everything about the murder investigation.

"It was Tim, wasn't it?" she guessed. "By the way, I knew Neil wasn't his real name."

I talked to her through Steve, because as much as I tried, I failed to materialise again.

"Maybe it's Tim who sparks off the right emotions to make you solid," she suggested.

I thought about it, recalling how he had been there both times. She might have a point.

"I never thought of that, but it makes sense," Steve said, reaching for a book.

This one was titled "Physical Manifestations of Spirits."

The two of them read the page he flicked to. I considered leaving. I didn't need to hang around for them to talk about me.

"I could help," Julia said as I closed my eyes, trying to decide where to go.

"Help?" Steve and I asked in unison.

My eyes opened.

"With the investigation. I have a cousin who works for the police. If we find something, we can get it to him. He'll make sure the right people see it."

"Why would you do that?" I asked.

"She wants to know why, and so do I. I'm not used to people believing me, much less offering to help."

"I get to help a ghost solve her murder and I'll save who knows how many lives from that freak. Why wouldn't I want to help?"

Steve smiled, but I noticed he seemed disappointed. The smile was forced and looked more like a grimace on closer inspection. He felt concern for her safety.

Chapter Twenty-Two

Julia spread out the pages she had torn out of the A5 notepad, piecing them together like a bizarre jigsaw puzzle. On one sheet was an image of Paul. Given the fact they had never met, the sketch wasn't far off the mark. I looked down at that face, the one I used to look forward to seeing. Instead of the persona he created of a loving and loyal boyfriend (and later, fiancé), I saw perverse desires in his eyes, and a mouth that existed solely for lies. He was nowhere near the level of obscene Tim had uniquely achieved, but I still berated myself for wasting so much of my life with Paul.

"So, he's ruled out. He's a perv, but not a murderous one," Julia said.

"Why does she need to go through all this? We already know who the killer is," I demanded.

"What's she saying?" Julia asked, not for the first time, as she saw Steve looking up at me.

"She said your drawings are amazing, and thanks for helping."

"Liar," I muttered, walking towards the kitchen area to avoid the urge to prove Julia's theory wrong by materialising, even without Tim there to make me angry — because then I would give Steve a good hard kick.

"Maybe move it along though," I heard him suggest. "We both know all of this. What we need to figure out is how to make sure the police get Tim for this."

I walked back to the living room area.

"Ssh," Julia held up her hand at Steve, while studying the rest of the notes and sketches. "This is my process. I didn't live this like you two did."

I stood watching over her shoulder as she picked up the paper which she had written, "more victims the first time around, a chance to stop them now."

"Was I killed the first time she came back as a ghost?"

"No, not you, some other women, but not you." Steve said as he threw me a look.

I could tell he blamed me, but it wasn't the time to argue, even if I had a valid argument.

"So, things have changed this time round and now he's after me," Julia noted.

"It's my fault," I relented. "We didn't go to the bar the first time around. Tim wouldn't have been there anyway. He was only there this time because he was meeting Emma about the I.D."

Julia opened her mouth to ask, but Steve cut her off. "She thinks it's her fault because we did things differently this time."

"Ah, cause and effect," she exclaimed.

Steve nodded, but the way his eyes seemed to search mine for an answer, suggested he felt as unsure about her words as I did.

Seeing his confusion, she elaborated, "it's like a chain of events. Think of them as dominoes all set up to go off. If something blocks the path, they might veer off in a different direction to either finish the alternative route, or stop falling altogether. One thing in the way is all it takes."

"So we blocked Tim's dominoes by taking the I.D and making sure the police got it, then he veered off into the bar to threaten Sarah's sister. While that was happening, Sarah steered my dominoes into the bar. Can we drop this domino analogy now?" Steve asked.

"Yes, but you get the point, right?"

"Yes," we both said.

"Sarah gets it too," he added.

"I wish I could talk to her directly," Julia said.

"I wish I could give you this so-called gift, but there'd be no returns," Steve quipped.

"That's it," she said.

"I can't give you the sight, or whatever you want to call it."

"No." She shook her head. "But I can still talk to her. Come with me to my flat. I have a Ouija Board."

"Haven't we all heard that pick-up line before?" I retorted.

Steve shook his head at me, then at her. "You shouldn't mess around with that kind of thing."

"I'm going to try contacting her whether you're there or not. So if you want to protect me from bad spirits or whatever, you should follow me now." Julia got to her feet and looked around as she put on her long red coat. "Sarah, if you want to talk to me, follow me home and I'll contact you on the Ouija Board," she called out.

I glanced at Steve before I followed Julia to the door.

"She's with me, isn't she?" She turned back to Steve. He looked at her, then at me – unsure who to plead with first, judging from the torn expression in his eyes and etched into the creases of his face.

"Why not?" I shrugged. "It'll be nice to have a chat with someone else. No offence."

Steve relented, grabbed his jacket and followed us out of the house, only stopping to lock the door after himself.

He tried to talk us both down all the way to Julia's home, but we refused to listen. I saw his face reddening and his hands twitching as he became more and more agitated.

"I'm not doing this to annoy you, I just think it might help for me to talk to Julia."

"Then talk through me," he replied, looking in her direction to avoid resembling a crazy person to passing drivers and their passengers.

I'm sure she picked up on the fact that he wasn't talking to her, but replied on behalf of both of us anyway. "It gets like Chinese whispers, talking direct is better. I'm sure Sarah agrees with me."

"I'll protect you both from anything bad that comes through," I offered.

"She says she'll protect us from anything else that comes through, but she won't be able to see it. Ghosts can't see other ghosts," he insisted.

"I've done this before," Julia admitted. "I understand what to do if a spirit lingers or seems maleficent."

Steve realised he was beat, residing himself to helping her set up the board in her attic flat, after we arrived there.

I walked around her attic flat, visually examining everything to make up for the fact I couldn't touch any of it. Everything looked antique; from the furniture to the ornaments spread across the top of a mantelpiece. I assumed the local furniture or home department store didn't sell them. An antique store might.

"Where did she get all this stuff?" I asked Steve.

"I'm not asking her that," he stated, his eyes wandering to the ornaments, lingering on a woman with a baby in her arms.

"What's she asking?" Julia wanted to know.

"She's only going on about the décor, like she's writing for a home furnishing magazine in the afterlife or something," he said, rolling his eyes.

"I wish I could materialise and shove that mother and baby where the sun doesn't shine," I retorted.

"Now she's threatening me. It's quite common though, for ghosts to become angry and…" a gust of wind cut him off, blowing a stack of papers off the desk.

Julia leapt to her feet, her faced creased in fear or confusion, maybe both.

I lifted my hands, despite knowing Julia couldn't see me. "That wasn't me, I swear."

"There's another spirit here. This is why I didn't want to do this Ouija Board crap. We haven't started yet and they already recognise me as someone with the sight. The board just makes them stronger," he protested. His hands covered his ears and he scrunched his eyes shut.

"Steve," Julia said, her voice softer than when she first insisted on using the board. She looked in my direction, then shook her head.

"Steve," I said, stepping forwards and trying to take his hands in mine. Of course, my hands slipped through like they were made of air. It might be better if they were. At least air is useful. I felt anything but useful at that moment — unable to help Steve in the midst of his turmoil. He battled his demons, more accurately his ghost, trying to keep it at bay. I tried to imagine what he or she might be saying to him. Did they need help too?

I almost felt like I did when I was alive and something would make me shiver for no reason. It was magnified by at least a thousand. My hands rested on Steve's, pulling them away from his eyes. His eyes opened and so did his mouth. He stayed like that, lost for words.

I looked down at my hands, but they weren't mine. The fingernails were painted blue, like Julia's.

"Oh God," I muttered, taking a step back, my hands no longer connected to Steve's.

I saw Julia stood in my place. She shuddered a little, but continued to stare at Steve. He was the first to pull his hands away.

"What did you do?" he demanded.

"I didn't mean to," I said.

He continued to glare as if I had sprouted horns and revealed myself to be the Anti-Christ. I doubt he could have hurt me more if I was alive and he punched me full-force in the face.

"It's okay," Julia tried to reassure him.

"No, it's not. She possessed you. Do you understand who does that? Maleficent spirits, that's who."

"Well, I'm sure she didn't mean to," Julia said.

I had to stifle a laugh. It was the same tone of voice my mum used when I was a child and I did something naughty, like taking another child's biscuit. It seemed like the wrong tone to be using when a ghost had possessed you just a minute earlier, accidentally or otherwise."

"Do you even grasp what happened?" Steve demanded.

"I was me, but I was her too. She cares for you a lot, but she thinks you might be happy with me. She's conflicted about it though. It felt kind of amazing, not the conflicted part, but the way I could almost talk to her."

Steve looked at her, his mind obviously processing everything she said. "You're crazy," he exclaimed. "Sarah doesn't feel that way about me, and you should feel freaked out by having your body invaded, not be proclaiming how sodding amazing it is."

"You don't get it," Julia replied, her voice much calmer than his. "She didn't mean me any harm."

"The fact that you're so easily possessed proves you shouldn't be around me at all. I'm a ghost magnet," Steve decided. 'For most people, the spirit works its way into their life through dreams and watching, unseen. It learns your strengths and weaknesses over time. You were taken over just like that." He clapped his hands together.

"Are you saying I shouldn't help Sarah, or that you shouldn't?"

"I don't know. Both?" Steve picked up his coat and left.

I could have followed him. I might have if Julia hadn't whispered those seven words.

"I still want to help you, Sarah."

Perhaps it was the way Steve stormed out, causing me to doubt his inclination to carry on helping me. Or maybe I was intrigued by Julia and how she might help, particularly as she had a cousin working for the police.

I walked towards the Ouija Board and concentrated on the pointer (although I felt sure it had a better name which I was unaware of).

Julia caught sight of it as I moved the pointer. I focussed on guiding it towards the letters.

H.I

She grinned. "Hi. Is that you, Sarah?"

Yes. That was easier, as the word was written on the top left of the board.

"How can I help you to get Tim arrested?" she asked.

Something easier would have been nice. I didn't know how to do that. Perhaps Steve might have been the better option after all. I looked at the door as I considered leaving, even though I could walk through the wall if I chose to. The fall to the ground outside wouldn't kill me, but if I struggled to ground myself, I might fall endlessly.

I.D.O.N.T.K.N.O.W. Just the act of typing out a few short words made me want to upturn the board. Talking would be so much faster, if Julia could hear me.

"I've got an idea," she announced. "Not about getting Tim arrested, at least not yet, but how we can talk to each other. When you possessed me, I felt and thought what you felt and thought. Maybe…" she began.

Surely she wasn't suggesting what it sounded like.

Chapter Twenty-Three

I wasn't wrong. Julia was suggesting I possess her.

I.C.A.N.T.D.O.T.H.A.T, my argument began – but with each short sentence of argument I typed, her idea became more appealing to me.

"I'm not suggesting you take over my life, but when we need to talk, you can share my body. Okay, that didn't come out like I meant it, but you know what I mean," she said.

It felt wrong, but I agreed.

O.N.L.Y.I.F.T.H.E.R.E.I.S.N.O.O.T.H.E.R.C.H.O.I.C.E took me ten minutes to say via the board.

"Great," she said, opening her rucksack and unpacking the sheets of paper which she had put together at Steve's house. She placed the board down, then sat on the floor nearby before shuffling through the papers.

I watched, uncertain how to help as she muttered to herself. I didn't understand most of it, but caught the occasional words like "first victim" and "type".

"He prefers women with dark hair as well as redheads," I stated. She couldn't hear me, I remembered that when the words were halfway out of my mouth, but continued to talk anyway.

"Redheads and possibly women with dark hair." She ran her hands through her own long black hair. "Not blondes, maybe. He didn't go after your sister with her bottle blonde hair, but he did try it on with her when she still had black hair."

That much was true. Though he might have been buzzing from his first kill when Emma went around there to pay him – and he tried it on with her – but he didn't seem interested in her at the bar. I felt like, even when Tim grabbed Emma by the arm, it was aggressive and threatening without the edge of sexual perversion. Her new look did nothing for him. He opted for Julia instead, with her dark hair.

I.A.G.R.E.E, I spelt out.

She nodded and looked at the papers for a few more minutes. "I'm going to the police station in Bolton. That's where my cousin works."

I followed her as she put on her coat and shoes, then made her way down the four flights of stairs and into the carpark. Without the board, I was unable to communicate to ask why she was going to talk to her cousin, what she planned on saying, or to point out he wouldn't be able to help. Surely if he worked in Bolton, he wouldn't be involved or even know anyone involved in my case.

I got into the car with Julia. She sat there for a few minutes, making me want to ask what she was waiting for.

"I'm assuming you're here, so I'm going to drive now," she announced.

I smiled to myself. She was waiting for me because she had no idea if I was already in the car with her or not.

"Thank you," I said, not caring that she couldn't hear me.

It didn't seem to bother her much either. She spent the journey talking to me about her life. By the time we arrived at the police station, I learnt she had a twin sister and their gran had died when they were twelve years old, leaving the attic flat to them both when they turned eighteen. Lilian, Julia's twin, chose not to live there. She insisted the flat and it's accompanying furniture let off creepy vibes.

I got a sense of how I must have made some people feel with my excessive talking when I was alive. It wasn't that I didn't appreciate Julia talking to me, but I wished we could have a two-way conversation.

She parked outside the station. I followed her inside

The man behind the desk smiled at Julia as we walked inside. Me, he ignored — as most people did.

"Long time no see," he exclaimed, walking around to the waiting area and throwing his arms around her. I had doubts over whether he was her cousin. The way he kissed her cheek as the two of them let go of each other, hinted towards them being a family who were too close.

"Is Toby around?"

Toby must be her cousin. That made more sense. I would have to ask her about the other guy later. He looked at Julia. His smile faded; his face settled into a serious expression as if he had something important to say.

"I'll get him."

"My ex," Julia whispered as we both watched him walk down the corridor away from us, with his shoulders slumped.

"He still loves you," I replied.

We waited a few minutes before what looked like a male version of Julia approached us from the same corridor.

His green eyes matched hers and his face was the same oval shape, only more masculine

"Julia, what's wrong?"

"Nothing. Can't I just pop in and say hi while I'm passing?"

"On the way to where?"

"Salford," she responded, clearly saying the first place which popped into her head.

"From where?"

"Denton."

"You're going in the wrong way. Did you pop in for directions?"

"No." She shrugged. "I need a favour."

"And it couldn't wait until tomorrow?"

"Tomorrow?" Julia's eyes stared at the ceiling as if searching up there for a clue.

"The meal for your mum's birthday. Are you okay? It's not like you to forget her birthday."

"I didn't forget. I'll be there. About that favour; a friend of mine was murdered."

"Shit, I'm so sorry. No wonder you're driving to Denton in the wrong direction."

"Yeah," Julia said, nodding. "So, I wondered, can you get me an unofficial update on how the case is going? I want to let her family know things are progressing. My friend would want this guy caught."

Toby forced a small smile. "I can't do that. It could get me in trouble or interfere with the case, or both."

"Relax, it's not even something you're investigating. It happened in Manchester. I'm just asking that if you find out anything from your friends, you tell me. I'm concerned this guy will kill again, or that he might be the one who attacked me the other night."

I guessed Toby hadn't heard about that from any of his friends, judging from his surprised expression. Julia had to give him a recap of Tim's attempts to make her into his next victim.

Unlike the policewoman who took Julia's statement, he sounded concerned, saying, "we should lodge a complaint."

"You'll be accused of being biased and too close to the situation," Julia said. "But I'm sure that guy would have hurt me if those people hadn't stopped to help. It was in his eyes."

"You've got great instincts. I always thought you should join the police."

As nice as it was to hear Julia talk to her cousin, I grew impatient, wanting to find out something that could help. I wandered toward the desk. Julia's ex returned, standing near the computer, though his attention remained on Julia and Toby. He looked so focussed that

I guessed he might be trying to lip read what they were both saying, from where they sat in the waiting area.

My eyes dropped to the computer screen. He was logged in. A file about dog fowling was open, but I had no interest in that. I wanted to see my own file. I focussed on searching through the saved files, unable to look up to make sure the ex was still distracted enough. I swore under my breath, unable to find anything that might be related to my murder; most likely because this station wasn't investigating my murder. It had to be accessible somewhere though, but how many other chances would I get to use a police computer unhindered? If I tried to use any other computer at a police station, someone less distracted than Julia's ex would notice weird things happening on the screen, assume computers problems and either restart it or get an expert to look at it.

I walked away from the front desk, catching the last of Julia and Toby's conversation.

"I can't promise anything though," Toby said.

Julia thanked him, then they hugged goodbye.

I followed her back to the car, wondering what he couldn't promise anything about. Was he going to try to find out about the investigation? Or had the two of them drifted onto an unrelated topic? I should never have tried to find information on the computer. I realised how stupid it was to think it would just be there waiting for me to access it.

I noticed Julia sitting in the driver's seat, making no move to drive away. She was waiting for me again. I made the radio switch on, to make her aware I was in the car. A cheesy pop song, sung by some squeaky voiced woman blared out of the speaker. Julia scrunched her face up in disgust.

"I didn't set it to this station," she said, switching the radio off.

I didn't care. I only wanted Tim to be locked up so that the whole experience of being there, but not being there might finally be over. I would find a way a way to cross over, or whatever.

Julia must have sensed my unhappiness. The journey back to Manchester was quiet. I could have travelled wherever I wanted without the car, but nowhere came to mind. That's why I stayed in the passenger seat, feeling like the investigation into my murder had stopped. There was nothing left for me to do. I never made it back to Julia's house. I found myself enclosed in darkness again, even though I realised I hadn't blacked out. I accepted it, throwing myself on the floor and deciding to stay there forever, if that was an option.

"What are you doing?" the God-like voice boomed.

I thought I might never hear it again, but I should have known better.

"I'm sitting on the floor, or whatever this is," I retorted. I ran my hands across the ground. It felt hard and cold. It was also the only thing I seemed to connect with as a ghost, without having to try. Every time I moved something, I used energy rather than physically touching it.

"Why are you giving up?"

"Because I have no idea what else to do. I'm dead and Tim is alive and he's going to kill again. The police don't appear to be any closer to catching him, despite everything I've done. How am I meant to stop him? Should I just haunt him for the rest of his life?" I grasped that was a possibility as I spoke. Maybe I would do that; follow him. Then every time he chose a victim, I might be able to stop him. The idea of having to witness Tim's every move was worse than the time my mum invited me to spend the weekend catching up on all the soaps she missed while she was away on holiday. Given the choice, I would opt for the soap marathon. At least none of the characters were as disturbing as Tim.

"You could haunt him for the rest of his life, if you really want to. Or you can stop him for good."

"Stop him how?" Surely he wasn't suggesting I kill Tim. God, or whatever higher power he was, wouldn't suggest such a thing, would he?

The darkness relented a little, partially replaced by what I could only describe as a cinema screen. I saw Steve in his house, typing something on his laptop. I heard a knock at his front door; the same loud confident knock that the police used when they called at my mum's house.

Steve jolted a little, then stood and approached the door. Whoever waited on the other side knocked again before he had time to reach it and peer out of the spyhole. The worried expression on his face confirmed it was the police.

"Steve Lowell?" the police officer who found the I.D at my mum's house asked him.

His partner, who had also been at my mum's house, was standing there too. The two of them stood side by side with their hands on their hips, like a human barricade in case Steve tried to make a break for it.

"Yes," Steve replied, his voice faltered.

"Will you come with us to the police station?" the second policeman asked. Although, his tone suggested that Steve had little choice.

"Am I under arrest?" Steve asked.

The scene faded before I could hear the response. Another image appeared in its place. Julia was being pursued by Tim again. This time it must have been the early hours of the morning; sometime between nightclubs and late-night takeaways closing and early morning commuters making their way to work. The traffic was scarce, and nobody stopped to help Julia as she tried to get away. Tim caught up with her and used her hair wrapped around his hands like a leash, dragging her into an empty carpark. I assumed he gained more confidence with nobody else around and maybe he even liked the idea of somewhere a little more open than an alley.

The scene fade, but the sound remained on. Julia's screams invaded my ears. They felt so close that I tried to see in front of me to check if she was there.

"What is that? Is that for real?" I called out.

Silence, before I stood outside Steve's house watching him being led into a police car. I knew if that was real, Julia's murder was real too.

Chapter Twenty-Four

Should I go to Julia to check if she was still alive? Or should I follow Steve to the Police Station? I supposed I could switch back and forth between them both, with my unlimited ghost energy. It occurred to me — I had been shown future events, then sent back. Maybe the rules changed again too, and I no longer had unlimited energy. I couldn't risk blacking out and leaving them both alone.

I forced myself to rationalise. The sun still shone. It was daylight when I saw the police on Steve's doorstep too. It was pre-dawn when I saw Julia pursued by Tim, then heard her murder. If things played out in the order they were shown to me, she was still alive. I hoped I was right as I slipped into the back of the police car next to Steve, after they bundled him in.

"You don't have to speak, but Julia is about to get murdered, either tonight or during the early hours of tomorrow, I think."

The policemen stood outside the car talking. The driver's door was open.

"Go to her," Steve mouthed, his eyes moving in the direction of the door to suggest I leave him.

I wanted to argue, but he was right. Even if the police thought Steve was the killer, they wouldn't hurt him. On the other hand, Julia was in danger, if I was right and she wasn't dead yet.

I arrived at Julia's flat as she finished drying her hair. The Ouija Board lay on the floor in the corner of her bedroom. She must have left it there in the hope I would contact her. I walked past the four-poster bed to get to it. What should I say? If I told her she would die around twelve hours later, she might freak out. I could promise to protect her. I had no intention of allowing Tim to hurt her, or anyone else. I knew what was going to happen. If I told her and she avoided going out, Tim would try again or go after someone else. If that happened, I wouldn't know when or who. I needed to let events play out as I had watched them, right up to the moment when Tim chased her. Then I would step in and stop him. Would I kill him though?

"Stop him how?" I repeated the same question I asked while trapped in the darkness.

I would just stop him, find a way to restrain him somehow, then Julia could phone the police and come up with a story to explain how she caught him.

H.I.

I let Julia know I was there.

"Where did you go?" she asked, unplugging the hairdryer.

I didn't respond, not wanting to lie, but what could I say? Julia stared at the board, waiting for a response.

T.O.H.E.L.P.A.F.R.I.E.N.D.

It wasn't an outright lie. Julia was a friend, and if I succeeded in preventing the scene I witnessed earlier, it would have saved her life.

"And did you? Help them, I mean."

I.H.O.P.E.S.O.

Julia accepted that answer and turned back to the mirror, scraping her hair back with her brush, before gathering it into a ponytail.

"It's my Mum's birthday meal tonight, so I'll talk to Toby again. I know he said he couldn't help yesterday, but I'm sure I can talk him round."

I moved the counter to yes.

She nodded before leaving me. Maybe she was assuming I would go to Steve's or do my own investigation, but I followed her from a distance. I had no way of knowing if her sensitivity meant she would eventually sense me if I stayed too close.

At least she wasn't taking the car that day, so it was easier to follow her. Even as a ghost, I doubt I'd be able to run after a car.

She caught a bus, forcing me to chase after the vehicle then throw myself through the back of it, passing through the engine and some teenagers sitting on the back seat. I landed on the floor of the bus, staring up at a baby sat on his mother's lap. He smiled and waved. The mother looked down, but didn't see me. I stood, smiling and waving to the baby, much to his mother's confusion as the infant giggled for no apparent reason. It made me question whether all the times I saw babies and young children seemingly talking to themselves, were they really just talking to someone or something that nobody else could see?

I almost missed Julia's stop and had to run off the bus the same way I had gotten aboard, only in reverse. I stopped in the middle of the road, allowing traffic to pass through me. One car steered a fraction to the left as if the driver sensed something, or perhaps it was the mechanics of the car reacting to my ghost energy. I hurried onto the pavement, not wanting to risk causing an accident if I could unintentionally mess with the inside workings of a car. This action brought me nearer to Julia as she stood outside a bakery. She twisted her neck to look in my direction but turned back a few seconds later. Her focus was on the birthday cakes displayed in the window. I stayed outside the shop, while she stepped inside.

She talked to the man behind the counter, then waited as he went away, returning with a box. Julia paid him and left the shop. Her hands held what I assumed was a birthday cake for her mum.

I stopped in the middle of the street, allowing her to walk away as thoughts of my mother filled my head. I would miss her birthday, I'd miss all her birthdays from now on. Julia rounded the corner before I realised I couldn't see her anymore.

"No," I said, running to the end of the road. I looked in the direction she had turned, but I couldn't see her. "Shit," I gasped. Could ghosts get out of breath? I felt like I was struggling to breathe, but I knew breathing was unnecessary for me. The feeling of needing oxygen was probably psychological. On the other hand, Julia did need to breathe, but she wouldn't be doing that for much longer if Tim had anything to do with it. "Tim," I realised, but the idea already turned my stomach, another bodily function I was no longer capable of.

I had no choice. If I didn't know where Julia was I couldn't protect her, unless I went to Tim's house and followed him instead.

I transported myself there. Part of me hoped he wouldn't be home. His bedroom wall boasted a new edition. He had bought a noticeboard, cut out articles about my murder and pinned them up like someone might do with their sporting achievements. To him, I was the equivalent of first place in a swimming contest.

"Talk about a cliché," I muttered, tempted to try ripping the board from the wall and smashing him over the head with it.

I heard water running. He was in the shower, but I resolved not to go in there. I would choose to be killed for a third time rather than see that freak naked. It wasn't my life at risk though. It was Julia's and all the other women Tim would go on to kill if nobody stopped him. I think that's the moment I made my decision.

I waited for the sound of the water turning off, then turned to stare out of the window, through the net curtains as the bolt unlocked on the bathroom door. His footsteps padded around the bedroom as he sang to himself.

"Tonight's the night," were part of the lyrics, but the tune was from a different song. He had changed the words. He was right about one thing though. It would be the night, although not the same night he had planned.

I waited until I heard the sound of him zipping up his jeans before I turned around.

The rest of the day was spent following him around. He may not have made up his mind about whether to try again with Julia. He returned to The Crusty Edge. I found it interesting that there was a new chef working in the kitchen, but no sign of Paul. That wasn't what I was there for though. I concentrated on Tim, as much as it angered me to spend so long looking at the face of my murderer. There was no remorse in his eyes, only insatiable hunger for more of the same. I noticed it as he chatted to a customer on the next table. She was a little older than me, possibly in her mid-forties.

"I've got to go, I'm meeting my husband," she said, leaving half her meal untouched.

I think she saw the same thing in his eyes as I did, even if she didn't fully comprehend Tim's capacity for causing death and suffering.

He made no move to follow her. Maybe he preferred people my age. I considered his would be victims. Julia was probably in her early thirties. There was a year or two between me and Shelly. From the pictures I saw of the other victims during my first time as a ghost, they were in their thirties too.

I felt sure I was onto something as I watched him try to flirt with a blonde waitress in the same age range, but he looked as if it pained him to do so. I figured Julia and I were right in thinking he targeted women with dark or red hair too.

Tim left the restaurant after a few hours and walked to a nearby bar, but found nobody to his taste there either, unless you counted the redhead at one of the tables. She snuggled up to her boyfriend. He was dressed in a leather jacket and jeans, taking up a lot of leg space. Tim must have decided against pissing him off by trying anything with his girlfriend.

I followed Tim as we walked a few streets away to a residential area, then stopped to sit on a wall. His foot tapped impatiently like he was waiting for something…or someone.

Some hours later, Julia emerged from the house across the road. I recognised the orange fake-leather jacket she wore, and her laugh as she hugged two other women. I wasn't close enough to get a proper look at them.

She staggered into the street. I watched as the front door shut and the lights in the house began to go off one by one, then I ran after Julia, determined not to lose her again. I couldn't believe her family would allow her to walk home at that time of night, even if she wasn't so obviously drunk? Hadn't the papers at least warned the local community that there was a killer on the loose? Of course, they published their articles about my murder. Nobody else had been killed yet. Most people prefer to assume these things are isolated and something that will happen to them or their loved ones, until it does happen.

I heard footsteps behind us as I caught up with Julia. She must have heard them too because she turned her head a little to the left, trying to see without looking obviously scared. She took a deep breath, then sped up.

"It's okay, I'm here," I said, hoping she at least sensed my spirit.

I stood behind her as she hurried through an empty car park, as if by placing myself between her and Tim I could protect her.

Tim breathed heavily from behind me. I turned to face him. He didn't seem out of breath, it was more like excitement at what he thought was about to happen.

"It's never going to happen, you sick fucker," I snapped.

The fear on his face as he took a step back, told me he could see me again. He definitely brought out the emotions which caused me to become corporeal.

"Sarah?" Julia asked from behind me.

"It's okay," I replied, not taking my eyes off Tim. He wasn't about to get away this time.

"You owe me an apology," I taunted him.

I wasn't sure if the way his eyes stared at me, meant he was surprised or scared. Then he smiled in a way that made his face twist with spite. I'm sure he was thinking about killing me again.

Chapter Twenty-Five

Tim took another step back when I returned the smile. He didn't realise I was dead. He couldn't kill me again, not unless I got brought back once more. If that happened, he wouldn't remember the previous time anyway. I don't know how he imagined I survived what he did to me, but I suppose the fact he could see me, outweighed whatever his head said. He was unable to grasp any other explanation.

"You like killing redheads and dark-haired women in their thirties, don't you?"

"What? I…I never, just you, but you're…so I didn't…"

"Are you going to finish a sentence today?" I asked.

"Speaking of sentences," Julia chipped in. "I should call the police."

I turned around for a second and saw she was fishing her phone out of her bag, before I focussed my attention back on Tim. I wasn't going to let him run off and kill some other woman. If Julia called the police and they showed up, without any proof, all Tim had done was to walk through a car park at the same time as she had. That isn't illegal. There was no way of proving his harmful intentions.

"It's not working," Julia said.

I hadn't intended to, but I believe I somehow blocked the signal.

"Good," I replied.

Tim made a move to bolt, but I ran the remaining few steps to him and grabbed him by both arms, pulling him backwards.

"I'm stronger than I used to be," I said.

"I don't understand."

"You don't need to." I pushed him on to the ground, face first and pinned him down. "I've been wondering about something. If I go into ghost form and pass my hand through your chest, then materialise, will it hurt you?"

"You're crazy," he exclaimed, causing me to stifle a laugh at the irony of his insult.

"Don't do it. You'll be as bad as he is," Julia pleaded.

I thought back to earlier, when I was in his room faced with his "board of achievements".

"I've made my decision. If I don't do this, we'll never stop him, at least not before he kills someone else."

I concentrated on returning only my arm to ghost form. As it was the first time I tried it, I felt surprised when it worked. Tim really did bring out the right emotions to help me transform so easily. I put my hand through his back as he shivered at the impact, then struggled to get free.

"Please," he begged.

He clearly wasn't enjoying this as much as when he was the one in control.

"Isn't that what I said? But you still killed me anyway."

"I'm sorry," he said.

I knew he wasn't remorseful in the slightest. Not for killing me anyway. His sorrow derived from realising he wouldn't be able to kill again and that the tables were turned. If he had the option, he would kill Julia and every other woman he took a shine to.

I concentrated on making my arm solid again.

"Arrgh!" Tim cried out. He twisted his head. Tears fell down his face by that point. Any doubts I may have had, slipped away when his face wrinkled in anger and he yelled, "fucking bitch, I should have taken longer to kill you."

I weaved my arm through him. A mixture of hard and squishy things pushed against it. I guessed they were ribs, and possibly his heart or other organs. It's not like I could see through Tim to know for sure. He jolted about on the ground like someone was electrocuting him. I hoped that's how it felt for him, but much worse.

Julia fell silent. I didn't know if she was still there, or if she had run off to find a phone to call the police from.

Tim stopped moving, his eyes widened. I retracted my arm which had become ghostlike again. Him no longer being alive, seemed to be the trigger that made me unable to control it again. Footsteps approached from behind me. I turned around to face Julia.

"Are you still here?" she whispered.

I didn't answer. There was no point; she wouldn't hear me.

"I found a pay phone and called the police. I know he was a killer, but I don't...I can't..."

I understood. She wouldn't have done the same thing in my position. There was a time when I wouldn't have either. Things change though. Like getting killed (twice), then wanting the chapter of my life where I was a ghost, to be done with. I just knew that if I killed him and put a stop to his killing, it would be over for me. I didn't know what would happen next, but I wanted more than anything for it to be over.

I stood, then looked at Julia. Her face was covered in white streaks where her foundation had been ruined by her tears. She turned away from Tim's dead body. Even knowing that it would be her lying there if he'd had his way; it still caused her distress to look at him. She was a good person,

"Death changed me," I said, unsure whether she would be able to sense me or my admission.

She nodded as if she seemed to get my point, even though she didn't agree with my actions.

"What do I do now? What do I tell the police?"

The sirens approached from somewhere behind us as if her words had conjured them.

"You'll think of something," I said.

I left before the police arrived at the scene. I didn't know how much longer I would be a ghost. Maybe I would go to hell, if it was all a test and I had failed it. If so, I had nothing left to lose; so I went to Emma.

She was at her own place. I realised the version of events I recalled hadn't happened. She never moved in with Paul, because Mum or Shelly could have told her about his secret hobbies. I watched her lying in the double bed alone.

I remembered what Steve said about people close to sleep.

"Hey sis," I whispered into her ear.

Her eyelids flickered, and she gurgled — opening her mouth as if she wanted to speak, but the words were lost to her. I watched her as she continued to doze.

"Why did you do it?" I asked. "Even if you wanted Paul that badly, that's no reason to hire a hitman."

Technically, Tim wasn't a hitman. He had only killed one person for money, but the use of the word seemed to have an impact on my sister She groaned and lifted her left arm before slamming it into the pillow.

"That's right. It's your fault I'm dead and you can't live with my death on your conscience." I wasn't sure where those words came from, but I carried on. "You're going to go to the police and hand yourself in."

"No," she mumbled.

'You are,' I said raising my voice, "because if you don't, I'll haunt you for the rest of your miserable life., which won't be that long."

Emma jolted upright, fumbling for the lamp and knocking it over. I didn't know if I would go through with my threat. Emma was a terrible sister for paying Tim to kill me, but she wasn't a killer herself. She probably wouldn't do anything like that again.

"Sarah," she called out, scurrying off the bed, towards the light switch.

As the room lit up, she spun around, her head moving left to right and up and down. I wasn't sure how she expected me to be on the ceiling, or under the bed as she got to her knees and peered underneath. She stood and flung open the wardrobe door. I took my chance to throw the bridesmaid dress at her. She bought it for my wedding to Paul. I only asked her because she was my sister and I had no female friends to speak of. She only said yes because our mum was in the room when I asked. I didn't know at the time that she was plotting to get me out of the picture and stop me marrying Paul, using any means necessary.

Emma grabbed at the dress and threw the garment to the floor, then stamped on it as if that would teach it never to throw itself at her again.

I looked around the room as Emma backed away towards the door. I spotted a photo on the dresser of the two of us as teenagers, on a rare occasion when we seemed happy together. I made it shake, but refrained from throwing it at her. I used the energy around me to lift it, so it floated slowly towards Emma.

My sister opened her mouth as if she was about to scream, but only a small whimper escaped as the framed photo hovered in front of her. She batted it away, causing it to fall face down on the plush blue carpet.

I focused on the light switch, throwing the room into near darkness, with only a street lamp from outside managing to force its beams through the gap in the curtains.

I heard Emma fumbling for the door handle, so I leaned over her shoulder and whispered, "tell the police everything."

She screamed as she found the handle and fled the room.

Sometime later I sat in the police station next to my sister. I followed her there, wanting to make sure she didn't change her mind. She was in such a hurry that she didn't change out of her pyjamas. She just put on her long red coat over them. Her face was pale; the first time I had seen her as an adult without makeup. If anybody thought her look was unusual, they didn't show it. I suppose they had seen worse though.

We waited there forty-five minutes before someone came along to talk to Emma. She told the man at the desk when she arrived that she was here to confess, but he had looked disinterested when he took her name and told her to wait. Maybe he assumed she was a drunk. She was dressed like a drunk, or at least I thought so.

"Miss Winters?" the young policeman asked. I saw the way Emma looked at him. He resembled a younger and slightly more rugged version of Paul.

"Yes," she said.

"You said you had something to confess," he said. His eyes fell to her pyjamas because she had unbuttoned her coat. I assumed it must be due to the heat, but as a ghost I couldn't feel the temperature.

The policeman tried to hide a smirk as my sister's outlandish dress sense.

"I paid a man to kill my sister and I helped him to frame an innocent man," Emma blurted out.

The smile dropped from his lips, and any sign of amusement vanished from his eyes. He shifted into serious cop mode as if someone had flicked a switch.

"You'd better follow me then," he said. He mouthed something to the guy at the desk, but I was following from behind them, so couldn't see to make any attempt at reading his lips.

Emma was led to a room containing a metal desk, with two chairs at one side and one at the other.

"I'm officer Karlson," the policeman introduced himself while signalling to her to take the solitary seat, then he took one of the seats opposite.

"Emma," my sister said, then I figured she recalled giving her name already as she added, "but you knew that already." She looked down at the table, then at the door.

"I'm just waiting for a colleague to join me."

Emma nodded.

That's what he must have been asking the man at the desk. I assumed that meant this was serious because he wanted another officer present. The door opened, and a policewoman joined them. It took me a minute to place where I had seen her before. Her lanky frame which hovered over Emma, made the policewoman look like she might be easily snapped in two. She was young; in her early twenties. Sophie, I realised. She was the woman who interviewed Julia.

I could only glare at her. She had treated Julia like she exaggerated the actions of an over friendly man trying a little too hard to get her number, rather than the murder victim she almost became. If she botched this up, I might go full poltergeist on her.

Chapter Twenty-Six

I didn't get to watch my sister's confession, or Sophie's reaction, because I was called back to the darkness.

"Okay, bring it on," I called out, stupidly clenching my eyes shut. I couldn't see, even with them open. I expected enough physical sensation to return to my body for the incoming hellfire to burn through my skin, or else what would be the point of my punishment?

"Open your eyes," the familiar voice boomed.

I did as he demanded and found that I was no longer submerged in darkness. I wasn't illuminated by the light of hellfire as I feared I might be either. I stood in a room devoid of any imagination as far as the decorating was concerned. The walls, ceiling and carpet were all white — to the extent that I felt like I might pass out or have a seizure from the excessive brightness.

The owner of the voice I had become accustomed to was sitting on a chair. It glistened silver, but the suit he wore was white, matching his beard and doing nothing to dispel the typical image of a god cliché.

"Is white your favourite colour?" I asked, wishing I had somewhere to put my hands as they seemed to dangle from my arms.

"I like to be consistent," he replied. "Take a seat."

I was about to point out I had nowhere to sit, when he clapped his hands. A chair just like his appeared in front of him, although I noticed how it was a little smaller than his. I walked towards it, eyeing the object with suspicion. How could it appear from nowhere?

"You've died and become a ghost twice now, yet you question something as simple as me conjuring up a chair? Everything is matter. It's less effort for me to bring the chair here than it was for me to send you back to three days before your death."

"I guess. Hey, I didn't say anything. I only thought that."

"You don't need to talk. I'm aware of everything that goes on in your head. Although I prefer to dip in and out. Much of it bores me. No offence."

I tried to smother all the swearwords as they seemed to gather and attack my mind. I thought about Paul and how I hated him, but not nearly as much as I hated Emma for betraying me twice, in two different ways. Even combined, that hate was nothing compared to how I felt about Tim. In those last moments, I understood I was doing what had to be done, but a small part of me felt happy, because I was consumed by anger and hate at how much he took from me.

The man chuckled, which unnerved me. I took the chance to get a look at the all-powerful being that passed for God.

"Don't worry, that always happens when people find out I can read their minds. The worse thoughts just float to the surface." He raised his hand, as if to demonstrate a thought rising up, I assumed. "I'm not God. I'm just in charge, but I'm not here to judge whatever you think your sins are. That's a different department, one you won't have to deal with."

"Same thing," I pointed out.

"I suppose it is. Now, onto business. You must be wondering why I brought you here and why I let you see this place."

I nodded, pressing my hands against the cold metal of the chair, enjoying the luxury of my skin against anything, no matter how cold.

"I won't be sending you back to your old life again I'm afraid, but you will have a new start. What you did was unprecedented; stopping a killer and getting your sister to confess to her part in your death."

"I killed a man and scared my own sister into admission."

"True, but you saved lives and your sister needed to pay for her crimes. The aptness of your work left me greatly impressed."

"Thank you," I responded. Was this another test? I wasn't even sure what the first test was, but I knew there was one. Had I passed or failed?

"You passed. Think of what you did as a job interview."

"For what?" I had struggled to find work anywhere other than in the restaurant with Paul. Why would the all-powerful life form in charge of the world, want to hire me?

"It's not a paid job. You'll get a room, like this to come back to at the end of your working days, or nights. The hours are quite ad hoc. You don't have to stick with white like I did. You can make your room yours, just by thinking about it."

"Okay. What is the job I would be doing?"

"I need a new Karma."

"What?"

'You didn't assume people get what they deserve just by chance, did you?'

I could only stare at him, unable to hide my confusion. I nodded while trying not to look stupid.

And that's how I became Karma, or more precisely Karma 1088 – meaning there are another 1077 of us, and someday they'll be more after me. We're the ones who find people and make them feel the way they've made others feel. If you're generally a good person, you've got nothing to worry about — but if you do more bad than good, I might run into you someday soon.

Epilogue

I sit here, transfixed on my target until my bum aches. I don't mind that part so much. At least I can feel again, even if it is just my aching bum. I'll admit I had no idea what to expect when God, as I like to call him, made me into a karma. It wasn't until the whooshing sensation exploding through every inch of me, turning into what I imagined electrocution felt like, when I realised I could feel again. I clenched my hands together trying to stop myself from screaming. Then it was over. I stood outside a white door. I opened it, peering inside to reveal a blank room. By blank, I mean that the walls were white and so was the floor. If I didn't know any better, I'd say the room connected with my mind. A carpet seemed to rise out of the floor, followed by the rest of the furniture.

I yawn at the thought of furniture, serving as a reminder of my bed; a king-sized divan with the perfect mattress. I would prefer to be there, but instead I have to watch my target; a man in his late twenties, with floppy blonde hair. He reminds me of a member of a failed boy band from the nineties.

He finally steps out of his car and strolls into the off-licence across the road from the roof I'm sitting on. I wait, my full attention on the door. When he reappears, he's clutching a bottle of something blue. I take a guess that it's alcohol for the fourteen-year-old girl he's been chatting up for the past few weeks. She thought he was seventeen and attending the local college. That last part is partially true. The boy band reject attends college most evenings...as a janitor.

Thanks to the television in my room which shows me what I need to see about my targets, I've learnt a few things about Larry. He's a thirty-something, unhappily married poor excuse for a man and enjoys talking to underage girls online, using false names and claiming to be half his real age.

I use the drainpipe to scramble down onto the street, then follow him from a distance. He headed towards a familiar looking park. Familiar because it's the place where I made sure my killer would never harm anyone else. Won't it be a coincidence if I give Larry his just desserts there?

A young girl sways on the swing as he approaches her.

"Teagan?" Larry asks, like he doesn't recognise her. He's spent enough time looking at images of her. She hasn't quite succumbed to the full-frontal nudity he's pestered her for, but she relented at sending him photos of her in revealing outfits.

"Yes?" Her voice is low before her mouth drops open in an O shape. She stands, takes a step back and looks behind her shoulder.

"Is everything okay here?" I question as looks at Larry again and she notices me approaching them both.

"Everything is fine," Larry answers for her.

"I wasn't talking to you." I stare at him until he looks away.

He takes in a greedy eyeful of Teagan as he walks towards me, moving his mouth closer to my ear.

"My daughter is having a strop. I'm trying to convince her to come home before her mother pulls all her hair out from worrying. So, if you could leave us alone, I'd appreciate that."

I have to give him credit. I might be convinced if I wasn't aware of his online activities.

"Your daughter?" I ask.

He nods. "Thanks."

"Don't thank me yet," I say, grabbing his arm. "Run," I instruct the girl.

"I wasn't…I didn't know. I thought I was talking to a…" Her eyes dart from me to Larry. Her legs almost buckle as she takes another step backwards and grabs at the framework of the swings.

"RUN," I yell as Larry tries to push me out of the way.

This new body of mine is stronger than the last and I barely stagger. Instead, I return the favour, shoving him onto the wet ground. He almost lands in a pile of dog muck, but hurls himself onto his shoulder to avoid it.

"Who the fuck are you?" he hisses, but I doubt he wants me to explain that to him.

"Karma and I'm a bitch," I said. Sure, it's cliché, but I haven't come up with a better line yet. I slam my foot down against his face, breaking his nose. His head hits the ground. He'll feel that when he comes around, but at least he isn't dead.

When I accepted the offer to become a karma, some of the others seemed in awe of the fact I killed my own murderer, exacting revenge in what they called a typical karmic way. I signed up to stop people like my killer and the guy who is laid out at my feet, bleeding from his head-wound, but I've never wanted to be renowned for killing anyone. I take out the phone from my jacket pocket and call 999. I tell them there is a man preying on young girls in the park. I give them his description, then take the memory stick from my pocket. I swiped it from him earlier when the train was crowded. He hadn't even noticed me taking it from his messenger bag, or all the previous occasions when I followed him.

I place the memory stick into his pocket. I leave the park, take the phone to pieces, then bin it three streets away as I hear police sirens heading for the park. Job done. I head home to my luxury mattress.

About the Author

Amanda Steel is a Manchester (UK) based author and poet. She regularly performs her work at various open mic nights.

She is also a podcast co-host and the editor of an e-zine. To find out more about Amanda's other books and projects, visit her website.

www.amandasteelwriter.com

CPSIA information can be obtained
at www.ICGtesting.com
Printed in the USA
LVHW112336120220
646801LV00001B/44